Easy

Does

It

D1488981

By:

Brooke St. James

No part of this book may be used or reproduced in any form or by any means without prior written permission of the author.

Other titles available from Brooke St. James:

Another Shot:
(A Modern-Day Ruth and Boaz Story)

When Lightning Strikes

Something of a Storm (All in Good Time #1)
Someone Someday (All in Good Time #2)

Finally My Forever (Meant for Me #1)
Finally My Heart's Desire (Meant for Me #2)
Finally My Happy Ending (Meant for Me #3)

Shot by Cupid's Arrow

Dreams of Us

Meet Me in Myrtle Beach (Hunt Family #1)
Kiss Me in Carolina (Hunt Family #2)
California's Calling (Hunt Family #3)
Back to the Beach (Hunt Family #4)
It's About Time (Hunt Family #5)

Loved Bayou (Martin Family #1)
Dear California (Martin Family #2)
My One Regret (Martin Family #3)
Broken and Beautiful (Martin Family #4)
Back to the Bayou (Martin Family #5)

Almost Christmas

JFK to Dublin (Shower & Shelter Artist Collective #1)
Not Your Average Joe (Shower & Shelter Artist Collective #2)
So Much for Boundaries (Shower & Shelter Artist Collective #3)
Suddenly Starstruck (Shower & Shelter Artist Collective #4)
Love Stung (Shower & Shelter Artist Collective #5)
My American Angel (Shower & Shelter Artist Collective #6)

Summer of '65 (Bishop Family #1)
Jesse's Girl (Bishop Family #2)
Maybe Memphis (Bishop Family #3)
So Happy Together (Bishop Family #4)
My Little Gypsy (Bishop Family #5)
Malibu by Moonlight (Bishop Family #6)
The Harder They Fall (Bishop Family #7)
Come Friday (Bishop Family #8)
Something Lovely (Bishop Family #9)

3

So This is Love (Miami Stories #1)
All In (Miami Stories #2)
Something Precious (Miami Stories #3)

The Suite Life (The Family Stone #1)
Feels Like Forever (The Family Stone #2)
Treat You Better (The Family Stone #3)
The Sweetheart of Summer Street (The Family Stone #4)
Out of Nowhere (The Family Stone #5)

Delicate Balance (The Blair Brothers #1)
Cherished (The Blair Brothers #2)
The Whole Story (The Blair Brothers #3)
Dream Chaser (Blair Brothers #4)

Kiss & Tell (Novella) (Tanner Family #0)
Mischief & Mayhem (Tanner Family #1
Reckless & Wild (Tanner Family #2)
Heart & Soul (Tanner Family #3)
Me & Mister Everything (Tanner Family #4)
Through & Through (Tanner Family #5)
Lost & Found (Tanner Family #6)
Sparks & Embers (Tanner Family #7)
Young & Wild (Tanner Family #8)

Easy Does It (Bank Street Stories #1)
The Trouble with Crushes (Bank Street Stories #2)
A King for Christmas (Novella) (A Bank Street Christmas)
Diamonds Are Forever (Bank Street Stories #3)
Secret Rooms and Stolen Kisses (Bank Street Stories #4)
Feels Like Home (Bank Street Stories #5)
Just Like Romeo and Juliet (Bank Street Stories #6)
See You in Seattle (Bank Street Stories #7)
The Sweetest Thing (Bank Street Stories #8)
Back to Bank Street (Bank Street Stories #9)

Chapter 1

Galveston Island, Texas
May, 1968

"Hello, there. We're Tess and Abigail Cohen," I announced. I was bubbly and smiling and full of nervous excitement as we walked into the jewelry store on the corner of Bank Street and 23rd.

"You should wait for Mom and Dad," my sister whispered from behind me.

I glanced at her to find that she was staring at me with wide eyes, looking intense, frightened. I wasn't scared, though. I was feeling empowered. I held my shoulders back and looked directly at the man at the end of the counter, the one I had been talking to when we came in. He was a large, older man, bald on top with dark hair that grew in a horseshoe pattern around the sides. The sparse hair he did have on the top of his head was long and it shot out in unruly wisps. I could see those hairs clearly because he had a bright light shining down on the work station in front of him.

He was hunched over, and I watched as his head came up. I figured he was looking at me, but it was hard to tell with the glasses he was wearing. They were regular wire-framed spectacles, but some sort of magnifying tool had been attached to both lenses, so I couldn't even see his eyes. I wasn't surprised to find a person wearing such a contraption, seeing as how this was a jewelry store and he was a jeweler.

I waved at him, but he didn't wave back.

He was looking our way, but I couldn't see his eyes and he hadn't spoken. He stared at me, stone-faced. He was so unresponsive that I assumed he hadn't heard me.

"Hello," I repeated. "We're the Cohen sisters. Tess and Abigail."

"I don't have an order for Cohen," he said, finally, still stone-faced.

Abigail pinched me, and I stubbornly ignored her, refusing to be intimidated. I approached the backside of the U-shaped counter where the man was positioned, and my little sister followed me reluctantly.

"We don't have a jewelry order," I said, smiling at the man. "We're the Cohen sisters. We just pulled into town like three minutes ago. My parents are a few minutes behind us. Our dad wanted to stop at the service station and get gas for their trip back home. It took us almost three hours to get here, and we didn't stop. He said they wouldn't spend the night tonight, but Mom might talk him into it, depending on how big the apartment is."

"That means *we're* sleeping on the floor," Abigail said from behind me.

"We don't know for sure if they're staying," I said to her.

"Excuse me, ladies, but none of this has anything to do with me," the man said. He used a no-nonsense tone in an effort to get our attention. I was instantly flustered and defensive because of his surly tone, and I stepped back, pointing upward.

"Upstairs," I reminded him, trying to smile. "We're moving in upstairs. We're the Cohen sisters. My dad's the one who worked it all out with you. We're your new tenants for the summer."

The man let out a scoff, shaking his head as he went back to his work. "I'm not your landlord," he said. "I have nothing to do with you or your apartment."

He was grumpy, and I held my head high, trying to show Abigail that we could take this whole encounter with a grain of salt.

"We rented the apartment above the jewelry store on the corner of Bank Street and Twenty-third," I said, looking hopeful. "It was my understanding that there was a jewelry store on the first floor, right below us. I thought this was the right place."

"It probably is the right place," he said. "But it still has nothing to do with me. I don't know any of the tenants upstairs except Joan. I pay rent here, same as you do. Your door's that way." (He pointed behind us and to his right.) "Between here and the hardware store."

And that was it.

He didn't introduce himself or say *welcome to Galveston* or anything. He just went back to his work, assuming we'd show ourselves out, which we did.

"I told you we should wait for Mom and Dad," was the first thing Abigail said when the door closed behind us.

I was unaffected by his grumpiness.

"So what if we went in the wrong door? I'm sure he gets that all the time. It didn't hurt him to tell us where to go."

I walked down the sidewalk in the direction the man had indicated, and I glanced over my shoulder at the sign for the jewelry store. It said McCain Jewelers, and I added Mister McCain to the list of people I didn't like very much in Galveston. He was the only person on it so far, but that wasn't saying much since he was the only person we had met.

I wasn't going to let that discourage me, though. Today was the first day of the rest of my life. I had never been to a city as far away as Galveston without my parents, and I had never lived on my own. Today, I was doing both of those things. But I was ready for this. It was my first apartment, and it was on a beautiful island. Life was good.

My parents would tell you this was a summer trip. They'd tell you that Abigail and I were just staying for the summer and that, come August, we'd be moving back home to Starks, Louisiana.

They were under the impression that we'd be moving back home because that had been the plan all along. Now that I was in Galveston, though, I couldn't promise that I would be able to stick to the original plan. I had dreamed of living on the beach since I was a little kid. It was like I felt homesick for the beach even though I'd barely ever been there.

I fell in love with Galveston Island before we ever even got on the ferry. I loved palm trees, and I wanted to get better at art and make paintings of coastal landscapes. I had already done my research, and I knew there was an abundance of beautiful Victorian architecture in Galveston. I wanted to become a famous painter, and this island was just the inspiration I needed.

I had whimsical dreams that didn't quite line up with my parents' plan of me marrying Stephen Matthewson and buying the house next door to them. Both Stephen and the house next door to my parents were fine options in the long run, but I had wild oats to sow, and my parents knew it.

That was why they had offered to pay for this summer trip. This was an attempt to show me that we had beautiful beaches right here, close to home. They set me up with a trip to Galveston to keep me from moving to California, but ultimately, they wanted me home, in Starks, Louisiana, population thirteen.

Okay, thirteen was an exaggeration, but it was a very small town. My graduating class had thirty-six students and Abigail's had thirty-four. She was twenty years old and I was twenty-two, and as far as my parents were concerned, we should both be married and having babies by now.

Abigail had her own version of Stephen Matthewson waiting for her at home, but his name was Bubba Landry. Neither of us were technically going out with these guys, but in a town as small as Starks, it was hard to avoid getting paired up with your most logical match. That had been the way things were since we were kids. Stephen was my logical match and Bubba was my sister's. We had gone out with them from time to time over the years, but neither of us had made any promises about settling down with them in the future.

Abigail was a lot more boy-crazy than I was. Since we were raised in such a small town, there wasn't much trouble we could get into. If one of us was more of a rebel, it would be me, but Abigail's weakness was that she loved to look at guys. She didn't break many rules, but if she ever did, it would be on account of a man. One of the main reasons she went to college was to see what her options were other than Bubba.

My mom happened to love Bubba, (and Stephen, for that matter) and she was convinced that this trip would be just the thing to bring us to our senses and make us realize we had everything we needed back home. I was already beginning to think her plan would backfire in spite of the lukewarm welcome from the jeweler on the corner.

I walked down the sidewalk on Bank Street until I reached a small, hunter green awning with a door underneath it. It wasn't marked in any way, but it had to be the right place because just beyond it was the edge of the next building, which was the hardware store.

There were cars parked on the side of the road, and two young boys jumped out from between two cars and ran past us, yelling at each other and playing chase. Their mother followed right behind them, apologizing to us and fussing at them. Abigail and I watched as all three of them rushed along the sidewalk to the door of the hardware store.

The whole scene was divine. We were used to living so far out in the country that there was absolutely no way two kids would run past our front door. I smiled and took a deep breath, relishing in the hustle and bustle and newness of it all.

"Those little boys nearly knocked you over," Abigail said.

"I'm fine," I assured her, smiling. My sister's hair was styled in a neat bubble flip, and I paused long enough to reach up and smooth a lock of hair that had come loose and was blowing in the wind.

"I'm just gonna put a headband on and let it go from now on," she said. "To heck with all this hairspray. Is it this windy all the time here?"

"I don't know," I said. "I was too young to remember anything the last time I was here."

"Yeah, I was only two years old, so I don't remember it at all," Abigail said. She was talking at my back because I had turned and was now fiddling with the doorknob.

I opened the door. I could hardly pay attention to responding to Abigail because I was so excited about the entryway. It was really just a long, wooden stairwell on the left, going up to the second floor, but on the wall to the right, there was hand painted lettering that said *Seabreeze Apartments* along with three mailboxes. They were hung on the wall in a neat row 201, 202, and 203.

"Ours is 203," I said.

"Yeah, but we're not getting mail here," Abigail replied. "Since we're just staying for the summer."

"That doesn't mean we can't get mail," I said. I lifted the lid on the mailbox marked 203 and peeked inside.

Abigail pulled me back by the shirt. "Don't, Tess," she said. "That could be somebody else's."

I turned and leveled her with a carefree expression while shrugging. "It's our apartment now," I said. "And there's nothing in there, anyway." My eyes widened excitedly. "Let's go upstairs."

We climbed the stairs to the second floor and walked to apartment 203, which was near the top of the staircase at the backside of the building. I had the key in my bag, and I unlocked the door. We walked into the living room and noticed that the apartment jutted off toward our right.

The living room was furnished with a couch, coffee table, and lamp. There was a hallway to our right and we followed it to the opening that led to a small, square kitchen. Just past the kitchen, at the end of the short hallway, were the doors to the bathroom and bedroom. The bathroom was on the left, past the kitchen, and the bedroom was straight ahead.

We walked into the bedroom. There was a bed in the middle of the room, along with a nightstand and lamp. The dresser was on the adjacent wall. It was a nice-sized room. The whole apartment was roomier than I imagined and it had high ceilings. Abigail brushed past me and walked to the bed, turning and collapsing onto her back dramatically.

"Don't get too comfortable," I said.

"Why not? I want to sleep in here with you," she said, propping herself onto her elbow.

"What? I thought you already said you wanted the couch. I thought you were going to make the living room your room. Remember?"

"Yeah, I thought I would, but that couch in there is stiff and small, and it's covered in plastic. I don't want to sleep in there. Plus, you know, if we have people over, it'd be better to have all our personal stuff in here."

I stared down at the queen-sized bed, and smiled at the way Abigail was sprawled out, taking up most of it.

"Come on," she said. "Just let me share this room with you. I'll just sleep with you."

My little sister had been afraid of the dark her whole life, so this was a phrase she had said to me countless times.

"What do you do when you go to college?" I asked, looking at her.

"You know what I do. You've been to my dorm. I have my own bed. I'm not asking because I'm scared. I just don't want to sleep on that couch… and you have all this room in here, anyway." Abigail stretched out on her back and moved her arms and legs like she was making a snow angel. The quilt bunched up around her as she moved.

"Fine," I said. I set down my bag and sat next to Abigail on the bed. I glanced out of the window before I swiveled to look at Abigail.

"Thank you," she said. "I won't take up any room at all."

I knew this was a lie since she kicked, but I also didn't mind having her in the room with me. I was a little reluctant about sleeping alone, too. Unlike my sister, I had not gone to college after high school. I got a job at Tillman's Pharmacy right after I graduated, and I had been working there ever since. I slept in my own room while she was away, but it was at my parents' house. This summer would be my first experience living on my own, and I was terrified and overjoyed at the same time.

Chapter 2

"Esther!" I could tell by my mother's sharp, urgent tone and the fact that she called me by my full name rather than Tess that she meant business.

I sprang off the bed and headed toward the living room as quickly as I could. My mother was standing in the doorway of our new apartment, staring at me with a wide-eyed motherly glare. "Your father needs your parking place," she said. "We've circled the block twice and can't find anything close."

I had my car keys in my pocket, so I instantly headed toward the door. I walked past my mom while she was still talking. "We found a spot down by the lawyer's office, but if we parked there, we'd have to make trips all that way, so Dad told me to come ask you to move your car."

My mother's station wagon was packed to the brim with our things. We would have several trips each, so I knew we needed to let my dad park as close as possible.

"I'll move it," I said, walking down the stairway once I made it past my mom.

"Your dad circled the block," she said at my back. "Don't get out of your spot till you see him come back around because somebody else will get your spot if you do."

I passed through the area with the mailboxes at the bottom of the stairs, and walked out of the door.

I glanced back to find that my mom and sister were following behind me so I paused and held the door for them. We all walked outside together, but they stayed back by the door and I instantly went to the driver's side of my 1963 Volkswagen Beetle.

It was light yellow, and I loved it dearly. It wasn't brand new when I bought it, but it was only a few years old, and the man I bought it from had taken really good care of it.

I had worked full-time and saved every penny for over a year to be able to afford it. Abigail didn't have a car of her own, and she thought I was the hippest big sister ever for saving up and buying it. She would move back to Lake Charles in the fall for college, but until then, her summer home was at the beach with me and my VW Beetle. I stood by my car, watching the street, waiting for my dad.

"He circled the block," my mom said, seeing me looking out for him. "Just wait till he gets here."

"I am," I said.

My eyes roamed over the neighboring buildings, and I took a deep breath, taking in the mid-morning air. It smelled different here than it did back home. The air had a different feel to it, too. I smiled, taking in all the buildings and cars. This was completely different than the tiny, country town I was used to. I felt resplendent in this city, and I stood up straighter than usual.

I saw my dad come around the corner. I caught sight of him from over the other cars and I waved big at him, letting him know where I was. He stopped in the middle of the road, giving me plenty of room to back out of my parking spot so that he could take it. I quickly got into the car to move it.

I was used to driving a standard by now, but sometimes I still had trouble. I had to push down on the gear-shifter and pull it toward me to get it into reverse. I felt around for the gears, making sure the shifter was in the right place. It was easy to miss the gear, which made a loud, embarrassing grinding sound.

I gave it gas slowly, smiling when the car moved backward without that sound. I let up on the clutch as I gently pressed the gas pedal, trying for that delicate balance that would let me back-up smoothly.

I watched in my rearview and glanced behind me, but the way was clear and I backed out easily. I drove forward to circle the block in search of another parking spot.

There was a small parking lot on 23rd Avenue, close to our building, but there were a lot of cars in it when I drove by earlier. I figured I could always drive through it if I couldn't find another spot on the street.

I was having thoughts of parking options when I heard a siren approaching. I looked back to find that a police officer was turning onto Bank street, and I watched as my dad slowly pulled into my parking place so that he could get out of the way. There was no traffic, so I crept along in first gear, watching the scene behind me unfold in the rearview mirror.

The officer pulled up and stopped behind my father. There was a second man in the passenger's seat, and he got out of the car, pointing and saying something. It looked like he was talking to my family. I turned and glanced over my shoulder, noticing a few people coming out of the hardware store.

I hurried and parked when I found a spot in front of the law office at the end of the block. By the time I got out of my car and began walking back toward my family, the officer who was driving had already double parked behind my dad and gotten out of his vehicle.

Several people had gathered in front of the hardware store. My parents and sister were there, too, but they were standing off to the side.

My heart dropped when I noticed blood. I saw a man holding a white piece of fabric on the side of his face. He took it off to readjust it, and I saw a flash of red blood. He was a tall, healthy middle-aged man who's only infirmity seemed to be the injury to his face.

"I'm the one who called it in! I saw the man running down the block!" an older lady yelled from an upstairs window, right above the jewelry store.

I squinted in her direction. I couldn't see her very well, but I thought she did have white hair, and her voice definitely sounded old—warbly and high-pitched. There were several of us standing on the sidewalk nearby, and we all looked up when she yelled down.

She continued. "I saw that man running off! I was the one who called it in. I was just sitting here, looking out the window, and all of a sudden, I saw that man come running out from under the hardware store awning and down the street like he was being chased by wild animals. I didn't think much of it at first, thought maybe he was just in a hurry. But then he turned his back to me when he was running up the street, and I saw blood running all down the back of his shirt. Enough blood to kill a man, I thought." She reached her arm out of her open upstairs window, and pointed. "He had a gold car parked right there on the corner."

"Yes, ma'am, Mrs. Harper. We were coming here to answer your call about it, but I've got Nathaniel King down here, and he seems to know what happened. I think they've got it under control."

"Oh, does he?" she yelled curiously in her little old lady voice. "What was it? Did something happen at the hardware store?"

I glanced at the man with a bloody eyebrow. He was shaking his head at the officer, and I got the idea, just from his expression, that maybe Mrs. Harper had a hard time minding her own business. I assumed the man with the wound was Nathaniel King. I also assumed that the hardware store, which was called *King's Hardware*, belonged to him.

I walked slowly and circled around discreetly to stand by my family so we could leave them alone.

"It's all fine, Joan!" Mr. King yelled. "We knew that boy who ran off, and we've already handled it. Thanks for alerting the sheriff, but it's all taken care of." He turned and began speaking to the officer in a quieter tone. "I wasn't going to call you," he said. "It was a matter between that boy and my son, and I had already taken care of it."

I could hear their conversation because they were only about five feet from my family and I had to walk past them.

"Hello, young lady." The man with the bloody eyebrow greeted me as I passed. It was an awkward time for an introduction, but he was just one of those guys who was too much of a gentleman to ignore a passing lady.

"Hello," I said, turning to him with a nod and trying not to stare at his wound. I glanced past him, into the window of the hardware store, and I saw that there was a group of five or six people standing right inside where I could see them.

There had definitely been some sort of altercation. Everyone was wearing somber, concerned expressions. There were a few other guys, and at least a couple of them were tending to wounds. There was a young guy sitting on the floor, holding a bloody towel to his nose and looking mad.

I tried not to stare, but it was difficult. I hadn't expected any of this drama or action, and it was a shock to have it suddenly unfold at my doorstep.

Just after he spoke to me, Nathaniel turned to the officer, "I'd rather handle this on my own, if you don't mind, Dale," he said. "It was just a little fight between my boy and that one Mrs. Harper saw runnin'. Daniel said he knew who the guy was. It was a misunderstanding between the two of them, but we have it handled, if you don't mind."

"Are you sure?" the sheriff asked.

"Yes, sir," Nathaniel said, nodding. "I was in there, talking to Daniel about it when you pulled up. You know how young men are—somebody gets their feathers ruffled over a young lady, and the next thing we know, there's bloody noses."

The officer laughed.

I shared stunned looks with my family as I approached them, and we all shifted slightly toward the door that led to our apartment.

My parents weren't in a hurry to go to my door. I could tell they were curious and cautious about everything they were hearing.

Nathaniel King told the officers goodbye and thanked them for coming before he excused himself and headed inside. The sheriff turned to walk to his vehicle.

"Does this kind of thing happen a lot around here?" My mom had been the one to ask the question, and it was loud and directed toward the policemen. It made me cringe. "Because our daughters are moving in upstairs," she added when they stopped walking and turned to her.

"Mom!" I whispered, urging her to stop.

"Is it a safe neighborhood?" she repeated, ignoring me.

"Oh, yes ma'am, it's fine. We don't usually have any trouble around here."

"We didn't until that boxing gym moved in," the lady said, still sitting at her window. "And since then, we had a bike stolen, and now this."

"That bike being stolen was a year ago," Dale said, looking up at Mrs. Harper. "And the boxing gym had nothing to do with this," he promised, looking at us. "My son and I go over there on Saturdays. Marvin has a free class for officers and our families." He paused and looked up at Mrs. Harper. "You know Marvin runs a tight ship. That gym had nothing to do with whatever happened here today. It was something between Nathaniel's boy and one of his friends. And they've got it settled."

"I've seen Daniel and his friends a hundred times, and I've never seen that boy around here before. And Daniel's been doing that boxing across the street. I saw him leaving there the other day without a shirt on. He walked all the way across the street half-naked."

"Miss Harper, with all due respect, we do live at the beach. If I had a dime for all the shirtless boys I saw running around this town, I'd be a rich man. I'll talk to Daniel about it later, and to Marvin, just to make sure it wasn't one of his guys, but there's nothing to worry about. Enjoy the rest of your afternoon." The sheriff squinted into the sun as he waved at Mrs. Harper. "There's nothing to worry about," he said quieter, looking at us again. He gestured across the street and we looked that way. There was a small sign over a door that said Bank Street Boxing. "Marvin Jones moved his boxing gym into the building across the street," he said. "It used to be called East Beach Boxing, but Marvin changed the name when he moved to Bank Street. Do you know who Marvin Jones is?"

My dad would be the one to answer, but even I knew who Marvin Jones was. He was an old boxer from the thirties or forties who was famous for his showmanship. I hadn't seen him fight, but I had seen moving pictures of him shuffling around, shadowboxing and doing fancy footwork to entertain the crowd. I knew he was from Texas, but I didn't know he lived in Galveston. I certainly didn't know his gym was right across the street from the apartment I had rented.

"The *real* Marvin Jones?" my dad asked, sounding impressed.

"Yes, sir," Sheriff Nelson said, proudly.

"He's been coaching here for years. He used to have a building over by the shipyard, but one of his students donated him this building last year as a gift for all of his community service. It's state of the art in there. There's a whole workout facility and even a regulation size boxing ring. Twenty-two feet, square. It's a nice place, and Marvin keeps out the riff-raff. He's a good friend of mine. Don't let what Mrs. Harper was saying worry you."

"Oh, we won't," my dad said.

"It's nice to know you're so fast to respond just in case our girls ever did need you," Mom added.

"Yes ma'am," the sheriff agreed, reaching up to touch the brim of his policeman's hat.

"This is Esther, she goes by Tess, and our younger daughter, Abigail." My mom was still talking even though the man was clearly on his way to his car.

"Nice to meet you, ladies."

I waved at him and smiled.

"We're from Starks," my mom added. "Over in Louisiana. It's on the Texas line, about three hours from here."

"I've been through Starks," the sheriff said. "I had a cousin who lived in DeRidder."

"I have a cousin who lives in DeRidder!" my mom said. "Shirley Trahan."

Dale shook his head, not recalling anyone by that name. He gave us a collective smile and nod. "It was nice meeting you, Esther and Abigail. What'd you say your last name was?"

"Cohen," my mom answered before anyone else could."

"The Cohens," Sheriff Nelson repeated, nodding and trying it out. "All right, well, welcome to Galveston."

Chapter 3

Mom and Dad stayed with us all day, helping us clean and unpack most of the boxes and bags we had brought with us. They thought about spending the night, but they ultimately decided to head back home.

My mother cried when they drove off, and I made a face like I was having a hard time with saying goodbye, but parting ways was always harder for the person whose surroundings didn't change, and in this case, that was our parents.

I was more excited than I had ever been in my life. Abigail's clothes took up most of the closet, and I was so happy that I didn't even care. My stuff took up most of the bedroom, anyway. The window in the living room looked out at the alley, so I set up my art station in the bedroom, which had a window that faced 23rd Avenue. I didn't have a ton of supplies, but I did have an easel and a few canvases and paints to get me started.

I was just happy to be living in a big city, finally. When I parked down the block, by the lawyer's office, I noticed a place called Carson's Diner on the corner of 24th and Bank. Ever since then, I had visions of myself sitting in there, hanging out, and making all sorts of friends.

Abigail was the boy-crazy one, but for some reason, I kept going back to what the sheriff said about shirtless guys and how he wished he had a dime for every one he saw.

I pictured a few of them in the fantasy of me in the diner. I'd laugh and talk and make new friends and crack all the best jokes at the best moments. I'd watch what I ate, sit up straight, and captivate everyone with my charm. They'd all wonder how someone so worldly and wise came from a little country town in Louisiana.

I was sitting on the living room floor later that evening, pondering these sorts of things. I was smiling and planning, and daydreaming about a glamorous future in Galveston.

I had my back propped against the front of the couch, but then I realized it would be more comfortable to go ahead and sit on the couch rather than just lean against it. It had been a long day, and sitting quickly turned to lying flat on my back, staring at the ceiling.

It was only seven o'clock, but we thought we might be in for the night, so Abigail had gone to take a bath. She went in there when a record was playing the last song on side A. I was consumed with thoughts, so rather than get up and turn the record over, I just stayed there, in the quiet, staring up at the ceiling and thinking.

"Get that cigarette out of your mouth, boy," I heard the man's deep voice say. He wasn't speaking loudly, but my window was open and my head was positioned right next to it. It sounded like they were just below me, in the alley.

"You smoke," I heard the other guy say. The man had called him 'boy' but his voice was deep. "First of all, I only smoke three a day, and I do it because I'm an old man. My body's broken down, anyway. It's different for you. Second, you don't talk to me like that, boy, I'll pop you upside your head."

I heard a slapping sound.

"Owww," he said.

I smiled and covered my mouth to keep myself from letting out a giggle.

"Seriously, Coach? You take it from me and smoke it?"

"You don't need this, boy. It's bad for your body."

"I know. I'm sorry. I just had the worst day of my life."

"I can see that," the older man said. "You're nice and pretty with that busted nose."

"Mom said once the swelling goes down, it'll be fine."

"I don't know," the man said. "Come here. Come see. Come over here and let me…"

He trailed off. I felt curious, and I felt myself leaning in, trying to hear their conversation.

"Oooouch! Cooooaaaach!"

"Hold still, boy."

"Oooh, oooh. Oh, geez, coach! Ooh, what happened just now?" the younger guy said.

"I just straightened it up a little for you. It's all right. It'll look good. You were a little too handsome before, anyway, if you ask me. We can't have you looking like a mama's boy the rest of your life."

There was a full minute of silence, during which time I slowly turned onto my stomach and then lifted my head above the low armrest of the couch to try to get a look out of the window. I wanted to try to see them. I didn't even care if it made me the Mrs. Harper of the back side of the building. It was an interesting conversation they were having, and I wanted to get a peek.

I did see them. Barely.

There was an older, dark-skinned gentleman talking with the lanky, young, light-skinned man who had been sitting with a towel on his nose earlier that day.

"Well, I came over here to talk to you about missing practice this afternoon," the older man said. "I saw where something happened at your daddy's shop today, and I wanted to hear about it from you."

"Yeah. Sorry I didn't go to class. I didn't feel much like fighting after I got my face punched in. And I didn't feel like talking about what happened."

"Yeah, but it's not just about you, Daniel. Your sparring partner was looking for you. He's counting on you to help him train. He's got a match coming up. He had to pair up with little Charlie."

"I know, I'm sorry," Daniel said. "I didn't want you to see my face."

The older man laughed. "You think I hadn't ever seen a busted nose before, boy? You knew I'd see it sometime."

"Yes, sir, I know. And I was gonna tell you, obviously, but I just didn't feel like going over there today."

"Your dad told me about it, anyway. He was talking about that friend of yours. He said Randall hit him on the back of the head with a glass bottle, and nothing happened—that he looked unfazed."

"It's true," Daniel said, nodding. "He had me in a corner, and Randall snuck up from behind him and busted him on the head. He swung it hard, too. I thought for sure he would go down, but he didn't. That scared me for a second."

"Your dad told me he fought off four of y'all."

"He did," Daniel said.

"Your dad was under the impression that you just had a misunderstanding. He thought he was a friend of yours who just got spooked because Randall misunderstood and hit him on the head. Your dad was telling me I should go recruit him for the boxing program. He told me he could be the next big thing."

"Maybe he could, but Coach Marvin, please don't. He's not my friend. I just told my dad that so I don't get in more trouble than I'm already in."

"Do you know that guy?"

"Yes, sir. Kind of."

"Did you do something to instigate that fight?"

31

"I didn't think I did, but I guess it depends on how you look at it. He wasn't coming over here to fight me. He was just coming for someone else… to ask for… I was taking care of it. If Randall didn't swing that bottle, there wouldn't have been a fight in the first place."

"Well, why did Randall feel like he should swing that bottle if that guy wasn't coming to hurt you?"

"Probably because he had me cornered. He was telling me some stuff. It might have sounded like threats or whatever to Randall."

"Were they threats?"

"I guess."

"Had you done something to provoke him?"

"Not him. I barely know that guy. He came over here to talk to me for someone else."

"Who?"

"Matty Stills."

"Now, why would you get mixed up with Matty Stills?"

"I wasn't trying to," Daniel said. "I played some cards the other night with Josh and Eddie and them. I've been doing that sometimes on the weekends. It's no big deal. But the other night, I lost big. That was the worst day of my life, until today. Anyway, turns out it was Matty Stills who covered my debt."

"And now he's trying to collect," Marvin said.

"Yes, sir."

"And your daddy doesn't know about any of this?"

"No, sir."

My sister came out of the bathroom humming.

I could hear her in the distance. I was already having to strain to hear the guys as it was, so there was no way I'd be able to hear them once she came out here and started making noise. I was just about to motion for her to be quiet, but the noise trailed off as she walked into the bedroom. I tuned into them again.

"What kind of money are we talking about?" Marvin asked.

"Two hundred."

"Two hundred dollars?" Marvin asked, his voice went up several octaves and his tone was full of disbelief. "What are you doing betting that kind of money, Daniel?"

"It wasn't all at one time," Daniel said. "It was over a whole night. I was up a hundred, and I had two pairs, aces and queens. Who beats that?"

"I don't care what you had, son," I heard a low thud.

"Owwww, ohhh!"

"I barely popped you," Marvin said. "And you deserve that for such a bone-head move, Daniel."

"I know."

"How do you plan to take care of this problem? Where are you gonna get the money you owe?"

"I get paid Friday," Daniel said. "I'll ask Matty if I can give him half on Friday and half in two weeks."

"If he doesn't agree to it, you'll have to tell your dad."

"Yes, sir, I know. I will. I'll tell him the truth if I can't get Matty off my back."

"You can start by calling him Mister Stills. That man is in his sixties. Criminal or not, people like to be respected. Now, you get on over there and settle things with him so you can stop lying to your daddy."

"Yes, sir."

"You need to take some time tonight to think about your actions, too. Understand that there's consequences to them, Daniel. Your daddy and Randall both ended up with busted up faces."

"I know. I feel really bad. Kenny got knocked out, and got his ring stolen."

"What?" Marvin asked.

"Yeah. Kenny came up and confronted that guy after Randall and my dad had trouble with him. Kenny had on this big state championship ring, and he bragged about putting a stamp of it on the guy's forehead."

"And what happened?" Marvin asked.

"Kenny got knocked out," Daniel said. "And then that guy reached down and took his ring off his finger."

"And your dad thought this was just your *friend*?" Marvin asked.

"He didn't see him take the ring," Daniel said. "Dad and Randall were standing behind Kenny when he fell, and they had knocked over a big shelf. No one saw him take Kenny's ring. I don't even know if Kenny knows it's missing."

"Well, don't you think you need to take care of that, too?" Marvin asked. "Don't you think Kenny will wonder where his ring went?"

"I guess so."

"Kenny's well over two hundred pounds," Marvin said.

"I know," Daniel answered.

"How big was this boy? Matty's henchman?"

"One eighty or so. I don't know. He's pretty tall. Maybe my height, and a little thicker than me. About Eddie's size."

"And he fought off all four of you?"

"He did. I don't know how, but he did. He hit like a sledge hammer. His fist felt like metal coming against my face… wrecked."

"Was it metal? Did he maybe have on some brass knuckles?"

"No, sir."

"Maybe he was holding his car keys."

"No, sir. He was fighting barehanded. I know because he was standing with his hands kind of open when he squared up with my dad."

"He squared up?" Marvin asked. "Did he look like he had boxed before?"

"Kind of. I don't know. He looked like a fighter and fought like a gorilla. It all happened really fast."

"How old is he?"

"I don't know, in his twenties. He's my cousin Jacob's age. They played football together in high school."

"So, you know him?"

"Yes, sir. I mean, not really. He wouldn't know me, besides being the guy who owes Matty."

"What's his name?"

"Billy Castro."

"I know that name from somewhere," Marvin said. There was a pause. "Do you know how to reach him?" he added.

"Which top do you like with this skirt? This one, or the white one I normally wear with it?" Abigail came out of the bedroom holding clothes on hangers and talking to me at full volume, and I nearly fell off the couch.

I had been so into hearing the guys' conversation that I forgot my sister might come into the living room at any moment.

"Shhhhhh!" I shushed her, but I did it more with my expression than my words. I barely whispered the sound, but my eyes went wide, like it was a matter of life or death.

"What?" she asked, looking concerned and talking too loudly.

I put my finger over my mouth before pointing at the window. "Somebody's out there," I whispered. "I can hear them, so if you talk loud, they can hear us."

"Just flip the record," Abigail said. "Or close the window."

"I will, but… it was that guy from earlier. The one in the hardware store. I think he got his nose broken during that fight. He was talking to someone else. It was two guys, and I think the older one might be that famous boxer the sheriff was talking about."

Abigail had come to stand next to me while I was speaking quietly to her, but she moved toward the window again when I told her who was down there. We listened closely, trying our best to hear them. Their conversation had been audible the first time, but now I didn't hear them at all.

My sister peered out of the window and waved, and I moved and glanced down there, horrified to find that the younger guy was looking upward, straight at us. My sister was standing shamelessly in the window, and the movement must have caught his eye. He stared at her for a second before waving back. She lowered the window and locked it, and the guy had already looked away by the time she did that.

"It was just one guy out there," she said, once the window was closed.

"Not a minute ago," I said. "There were two guys. They had a whole conversation."

"Did you hear it?"

I nodded absentmindedly, thinking of all the juicy things I heard.

It was no wonder Joan Harper stayed at her window.

Chapter 4

Abigail and I got an early start the following morning—our first official day in Galveston. We helped each other style hair and choose outfits. Both of us had brown-ish hair. Abigail's was a little lighter and curlier than mine, but both of us would be classified as having dark hair and eyes. We got that from our dad.

We headed for the beach first thing that morning. I brought a sketch book with me, and I made a rough drawing of Abigail sitting on a towel on the sand. I would transfer it onto canvas and paint it later.

I wasn't an accomplished artist, but I had a little natural talent, and I worked on it a lot. I had practiced every day for months, and I felt like I was finding my footing as far as working with paint, but I was still searching for my muse. My paintings didn't always come out like I envisioned, but I was getting better. It was something I enjoyed, and I was convinced that if I kept at it, my skills could one day catch up to my imagination.

I made notes of shadows and colors on the drawing of my sister so that I could try to bring it to life once I sat down with it at the apartment.

The sketch only took about a half-hour, and for the remainder of the morning, Abigail and I walked around and hung out on the boardwalk and down on the beach. We talked to several groups of people along the way, but most of the time, it was just short exchanges of small talk about what a nice day it was.

It was just before noon when we made friends with a couple of guys named Derek and John. We talked to them for an hour or so. They were locals, and they seemed nice, so we made plans to see them again that evening.

We told them we'd meet them at 7pm at Carson's Diner since it was close to our apartment. We had plans to 'cruise the seawall' with them, which was apparently something the locals did on weekends.

Abigail and I didn't hesitate to agree to go with them. I assumed we were just going to drive around. I had no idea what we would actually do, but *cruising the seawall* sounded like just about the best thing I could think of doing on a Friday night.

I had never liked using hairspray, but Abigail was just coming around to the idea of not teasing her hair. She put hers up in a high-ponytail to keep it out of her way while we were driving around, and I kept mine down and wore a headband. It was mostly straight and it hung past my shoulders. I took a ponytail holder with me in my purse, just in case.

I wore red, knee-length knickers with black flats and a small sleeveless floral blouse. Abigail wore a dress. She was comfortable in dresses, and that was reflected in her appearance when she wore them. She seemed happy and casual in a dress, and she wore them more than half the time. Our mom had gotten into sewing them for her, so Abigail had a lot to choose from, and they all fit her well.

We were so excited about having something to do that evening that we were dressed and ready to go at six o'clock.

"We could go eat at the diner," I said.

"Aren't we doing that with Derek and John?" Abigail asked. "I thought that was the whole reason we were meeting them at the diner."

"No, we're just meeting them there because I didn't want to lead them straight to our apartment— you know, just in case they're weird-o's."

"Oh, good idea," she said. "I never thought of that."

"Dad only said it twenty times."

"I know, but I thought he was talking about bad people or whatever."

"That's the whole point. Sometimes you don't know if someone's bad."

"Yeah, but not John and Derek," she said.

She was probably right. They were a little dorky, to be honest. They were friends turned roommates who grew up here in Galveston. They were on the timid side and had barely worked up the nerve to approach us when we met earlier. They asked if we wanted to go 'cruising the seawall' with them, and something about their innocent excitement made me feel like it would be their first time. I didn't say as much to my sister. Neither Abigail nor I seemed especially attracted to them, but they were nice, wholesome guys, and it was fun to have plans.

"I wasn't planning on eating with those guys," I said. "I was going to eat before we met them. We can eat something here, or go down to the diner early, but either way, I wanted to eat first. I don't want them to pay for our dinner or anything."

"Okay, that's probably good," Abigail said, nodding. She was the one who had been on her own for two years, but it seemed I was more comfortable making plans and taking charge, and Abigail was content to go along for the ride. Maybe it was because she felt like Galveston was my thing.

***

Abigail and I went to the diner early so that we could eat and be done by the time the guys got there. We sat at a small table near a row of booths.

The restaurant was about half-full when Daniel with the broken nose from the hardware store came in with the man I believed to be Marvin Jones. I knew he was the famous boxer now that I saw him from this distance. He was a lot older than the man I saw shadow boxing in those videos, but I recognized his kind face instantly. He had eyes that squinted just the right way that made him look sweet and approachable.

They sat at a booth that was near us, and my heart sped up with excitement. They were close by and I was positioned where I was looking toward their table. I wasn't nervous because I was interested in Daniel. He was handsome (as far as I could see past the broken nose), but he seemed younger than me, and honestly, it just wasn't about that. It wasn't about me being starstruck by Marvin Jones, either. He was just a nice old man.

I was intrigued by Daniel's whole situation, though, and I wondered if I would get to hear a continuation of the conversation I overheard in the alley the day before.

"Hey, Mister Jones, Daniel, I'll be with y'all in just a minute." Our waitress spoke to them as she brought our drinks to the table.

Marvin Jones gave her a patient nod. "We're in no hurry, Diane, we're waiting on somebody else."

Diane delivered our drinks and took our order. Abigail chose the club sandwich and I ordered the meatloaf. We were sitting close enough to Marvin and Daniel that they heard my order, and Marvin shot me a look of approval, which made me glance at him and smile. I liked that man instantly. I could tell just from a few seconds of eye contact.

Diane turned to speak to them, and Marvin shifted to stare up at her. "Can I bring you some coffee while you wait?" she asked him.

"Sure," Marvin said.

"What happened, did you lose a boxing match?" she asked, looking at Daniel.

"He sure did," Marvin said, answering for him.

"Do you want some coffee, too, Daniel?" Diane asked.

"No, ma'am. I'll have a root beer if you don't mind."

She nodded. "I'll be right back with those."

"Did you see that little yellow Beetle parked in front of the store?" Daniel said. "Laney wants one just like that. She's been begging dad for one like that since it showed up yesterday."

"Your little sister?" Marvin asked in a disbelieving tone. "Is she driving already?"

"No, sir, not yet, but almost. She just turned fifteen, and she's already begging Mom and Dad for a car. She saw that one parked outside the hardware store."

"Is she working there now?"

"Just since Alice quit. They're trying to hire a replacement, and Dad told Laney she needed to help out while we're looking for someone, and then she has to train the new girl on register. He said if she wants a car that bad, she needs to save some money."

Abigail and I shared subtle conspiratorial glances while Daniel was talking. I had been on the verge of saying something to them about the Beetle being mine, but I kept my mouth shut.

My sister pointed out a jukebox, which was near the door. I was thankful of that because just then, a dark-haired young man walked in. I knew it was the guy they were waiting for before he even headed to the booth.

It was the one they called Billy, I just felt it. This had to be the guy who had come to collect a debt from Daniel. It had to be the same guy who had a bottle cracked over his head and then took on four men, knocking one of them out.

He was a substantially large young man, but I had pictured someone who was almost as broad as he was tall. This guy was lean and muscular. He was dangerous, and it was obvious from the second I saw him. He was stone cold, not even sparing glances at the people he passed on his way. He headed straight to Marvin and Daniel's booth.

I did my best to act normal and ignore him, but I was mesmerized. I tried to make my glance at the jukebox look natural, but I found myself staring for too long, so I turned to my sister again.

"I might get a soda when she comes back," I said, making the most generic conversation I could.

"Me too," Abigail said. "I should have gotten one earlier."

She was as distracted by the table next to us as I was. We both spoke a minimum amount since we were paying attention to other things.

I tried not to look directly at Billy as he came toward the table, but I couldn't help but take a glance or two. Okay, I took three glances, but he was devastatingly handsome. He had a cut on his cheekbone from the fight the day before and his short, dark hair was combed away from his face.

He had on jeans and a white t-shirt with black boots. His face was noble and handsome even though he was straight-faced, almost scowling. His stride was long and determined. He was fierce and unrelenting, and my heart pounded. I was scared to death of him and yet, at the same time, I wanted to curl up next to him and see what he smelled like.

I took a sip of the water that was sitting in the glass in front of me, trying my best to ignore him. It was difficult because he came to stand in the aisle beside me. Daniel had been sitting across from Marvin, but he moved, positioning himself in the booth next to Marvin and across from the new guy.

Abigail was looking their way when he sat down. He must have looked back at her because she smiled shyly in that direction before glancing at me.

She adjusted her legs under the table, letting her foot accidently hit mine. I had no idea what she was thinking, but there was definitely conspiratorial foot-bumping.

Marvin reached out to greet the guy who just walked up. "I'm Marvin Jones," Marvin said, sticking his hand out.

"Billy Castro," the guy replied, shaking Marvin's hand. He didn't look like he was excited to be there. I wasn't looking straight at him, but I could tell by his tone and demeanor that he wanted to get to the point.

"Sit down, son, and I'll buy you some dinner."

"I'm not hungry."

As he was saying that, Diane walked up with their drinks.

"I like your shoes." I leaned in and spoke quietly to my sister. It was a bogus comment, and she knew it.

"Thank you," she said, knowing exactly what I was doing. "I got them like two birthdays ago from that store in Beaumont."

I nodded, but I was really paying attention to the action at the booth next to us, as was my sister.

Marvin asked for three orders of meatloaf, and Billy insisted that he wasn't hungry.

"Did you eat already?" Marvin asked.

"No."

"Then let me buy you a meal," Marvin said. "I wanted to ask for a few minutes of your time, anyway. You might as well fill your stomach while you're sittin' here."

"All right," Billy agreed, sounding somewhat reluctant.

"Three meatloafs," Diane said. "Are mashed potatoes and green beans okay?"

"I'll have mac-and-cheese instead," Daniel said.

"Instead of the mashed potatoes?" Diane asked.

"Instead of the green beans," Daniel said.

"And for you to drink?" she asked, talking to Billy.

"Water," he said.

Diane walked off, glancing at our table but not stopping to talk to us.

"I appreciate you meeting me here tonight, Billy," Marvin said.

"Look, I'm just trying to get Matty's money back. Daniel told me that's what we were doing here. It's nice meeting you and everything, but I wasn't coming for dinner."

"How much do we owe Matty?" Marvin asked.

"Two hundred," Billy said.

"What about the ring?" Marvin asked.

"What ring?" Billy asked.

"The one you took off of Kenny's finger."

"You mean the one he threatened to dent my forehead with?" Billy asked. "I'm keeping it. Matty expects me to collect, and that's what I'm going to do. If I can't get King Hardware over here to cough-up what he owes, I'll give Matty the ring."

"Nobody's trying to get out of paying what they owe," Marvin said.

"I already told him that," Daniel said.

"Listen, I didn't go in there planning on taking your friend's jewelry, but he came to me talking big, saying he was about to bury his fist in my face and other reckless stuff like that. You have to learn you can't go around talking like that."

"Kenny's got at least fifty pounds on you," Marvin said. "And he's an athletic enough guy."

"Yeah, but he was slow. He tried to throw a punch at me, and then he was just standing there with his hands down. It was basically a sucker punch with how slow that guy was. He deserved it, too. I was just trying to talk to Daniel, and they came in, trying to kill me. I had to get ten stitches. And not at a hospital, either. They got done in Matty's kitchen by a guy called Crazy Ray. As far as I'm concerned, after the night I had last night, somebody owes me that ring."

Chapter 5

The men sitting next to us at the diner were having what seemed to be a private conversation. But they had it in such a casual way that it was like they had nothing to hide. I had already told Abigail some of what I heard out of the window the day before, so she knew a little about what was going on. I was thankful she seemed as keen on listening to what they were saying as I was.

She and I continued our sporadic, meaningless conversation while the guys talked just to make it seem like we weren't listening to them. We did that for a few minutes before our dinner came. We were quiet as we began to eat our food, which made it easier to listen without feeling bad about it.

"I mentioned Kenny being a big guy because Nathaniel King said you knocked him out with a straight jab," Marvin said.

"I just punched the guy in the jaw," Billy said. "He wanted to talk like he was about to kill me, and then he came at me swinging, so I figured he needed to take a little nap."

"Nathaniel King also said you squared up with him. He said you looked like you were in a boxing stance. Do you box?"

"I fight," Billy said. "I assume that's the same thing."

"It is, and it's not," Marvin said. "Has anybody ever shown you how to stand, how to swing, how to block... those types of things?"

"You know what showed me how to stand and swing and block? Getting knocked out. Getting beat up. That's what taught me how to be faster and better. So, to answer your question, yes, people did show me how. They were fighting against me and not for me, but I learned, either way."

"What about Matty?" Marvin asked.

"What about him?" Billy returned.

"Does he fight for you?"

"He doesn't fight against me," Billy said.

"What's your relationship to him?"

"What's that mean?"

"Do you just work for him, or do you know him personally?" Marvin asked.

"I don't owe you an explanation about my relationship with Matty. I work for him, and that's all you need to know. Daniel gives me the money he owes, and I give it to Matty."

"I'm going to cover the two hundred for Daniel." Marvin said. "I brought that with me today. He'll pay me back for that later. I'll also need Kenny's ring back. I'll give you fifty for it, and that's the best you're gonna get. I'm not trying to get Sheriff Nelson involved, but I'd like to see that Kenny gets it back."

"I'll take fifty for it," Billy said. He looked at Daniel. "But you need to tell your boys to calm down. I was just over there trying to talk to you."

"I know," Daniel said. "I didn't know Randall was going to do that with the bottle."

"Do you have the ring on you?" Marvin asked, keeping them on track.

"It's in my pocket."

"All right," Marvin said. "You give me the ring, I'll give you two-fifty. And as far as I'm concerned, we never talk about any of this again."

"Sounds good to me," Billy said.

He reached into his pocket and pulled out the ring, letting it fall gently on the table in the space between them. I heard it clang—the low sound of heavy metal hitting the wood and linoleum.

With the way our table was sitting catty-corner, the boys were positioned in front of me and to my right. I wasn't staring straight at them, but I could see their movements in my periphery, and I knew what was going on. Marvin took a wad of cash out of his front pocket and set it down on the table, exchanging it for the ring. Billy reached out and took the cash.

"That was easy enough," Billy said. "We could have skipped the fight yesterday and the meatloaf."

"Why would we want to do that?" Marvin asked. "The meatloaf, I mean. A man's got to eat, after all."

Billy looked around impatiently as if wondering how long their food would take.

"She's on her way over here with the food," Marvin assured him. "And while we eat, I'll tell you the real reason I brought you here."

Diane walked up before anyone could speak. She gave them their plates.

"Wow," I said to my sister, almost silently but with excited eyes. I got away with talking about the guys because everyone at their table was preoccupied with their order arriving.

"I know," she said. "We don't have anything this good in Starks."

I had to work to hold in a laugh at her statement. I took a bite of food. It tasted good, but I was thinking of other things and didn't really care what I was eating.

Marvin thanked Diane and told her everything looked delicious. The guys took a minute to eat in silence before Marvin said, "Listen, I fight same as you do, Billy. For some of us, it's in our blood. The good Lord made some of us warriors, and that's just the way of things. You even said that you already consider yourself a fighter."

I ate bites of my dinner, listening to Marvin's every word.

"Are you trying to get me to fight in a boxing match?"

"No. Not yet at least. I just wanted to see if I could wrap your hands and get you to hit a few rounds on pads for me, that's all. I wanted to check out that straight jab Nathaniel was talking about."

"I'm checking it out right there on his face," Billy said, pointing at Daniel and his broken nose.

"I'm talking about you coming over to my gym. Give me an hour of your time and let me put you through a little workout. If you're born to be a warrior, you might as well channel it, son. You might as well see how far it can take you—do something for yourself with it. People make a good living fighting. I'm one of them. I'm not trying to make you any promises because I haven't even seen what you got. But I'd be interested in working with you for a few minutes. Just so we can try each other out."

"I don't see myself being a boxer for a job, and I don't really get into situations where I… lose fights. So, I don't see a point in taking lessons."

"Okay, well, if you change your mind, which I hope you do, you can meet me at my gym at nine o'clock tomorrow morning."

"Tomorrow is Saturday," Billy said.

"Yes, it is," Marvin agreed.

Billy took another bite of food, thinking. "I can't promise anything," he said, finally.

"I wish you'd come," Marvin said.

Billy stood up. He had been eating fast, and he had finished before I was even halfway done with my plate. "I'll think about it, but nine's early." Billy took some cash out of his pocket and began sifting through it.

"Don't," Marvin said. "I got this. I'm the one who invited you here."

"All right, well, it was nice meeting you. We'll see you around."

Billy turned to walk away. He glanced at my sister and then at me. I knew exactly where he looked because my eyes were fixed on him the whole time. His gaze locked with mine as he turned to walk out of the diner. I followed him as far as I could without blatantly turning and staring at him from over my shoulder.

I was instantly hooked.

I did not want him to walk out of the door.

I thought there was a serious possibility that I would never see him again, and I actually felt urgent and desperate at the thought.

There was no way I was going to stand up and go after him, though, so I settled for staying quiet and still and shaking off the feeling.

"He didn't even say 'thank you'," Daniel said once Billy walked away. "You offered him a free boxing lesson and paid for his dinner, and he just walked off without saying 'thank you' one time."

"Saying 'thank you' is hard for some people. Some people just haven't been taught, and for others, it's difficult. It takes a certain amount of humility and confidence to say 'thank you', Daniel. It's a little different for you because you were raised in a family where manners were required. You understand that it's the kind thing to do. But someone like Billy doesn't see it that way. Subconsciously, he probably sees it as showing he's weak. A 'thank you' from him would be like him admitting he needed or wanted something from me. It takes confidence to show gratefulness, and he's just not there yet."

"Not there yet?" Daniel asked, letting out a little laugh. "If there's one thing that guy doesn't need more of, it's confidence."

"Yeah, but it's not the same kind I'm talking about, Daniel. That stuff you're seeing is fake."

Daniel thought about that before saying, "It doesn't seem fake."

"I think I remember that boy's name from years ago. I don't know if it's the same people, but I think it might be. It seems right, now that I know he's mixed up with Matty. If that's the case, he hadn't had the easiest upbringing."

"What happened?"

"Just something from years ago. Some family stuff. If it's the same boy, I think his daddy might've gotten killed."

"I wonder what time they'll get here," Abigail said, leaning in and still making small talk with me so that it wasn't completely obvious that we were listening to the conversation at the other table.

"I wonder what time it is now," I said.

I looked over my shoulder, searching for a clock, but really, I was happy to have the excuse to turn around and glance toward the door at Billy. He was already outside, walking on the sidewalk, when I turned. I stared at him for a second or two and actually debated about whether or not I should stand up and run after him. *But that was just crazy. What would I say to him if I did that? Nothing.* It was silly of me to even consider trying to catch him, and I smiled inwardly as I turned back around.

"You didn't even look at the clock," Abigail said. She gestured to the wall to her right where there was a big clock with the picture of a vanilla ice cream cone in the middle.

It was 6:50.

"I guess they'll be here in ten minutes," I said.

"What do you think of that meatloaf, young lady?"

Marvin was looking past Daniel, and his voice was projecting toward me. I looked their way, and Daniel pushed his plate to the other side of the table before slipping from one side of the booth to the other.

"Yes, sir, I love it," I said, answering Marvin's question. "It's just like my mama's."

"I'd like to know your mama," Marvin said.

"She's my mama, too," Abigail said.

"Sisters," Marvin said, smiling and nodding as he glanced Abigail's way. With the way he was sitting, he had an easier time making eye contact with me, so he had to turn a little to face Abigail.

"If I'm not mistaken, you're the ones who drive that little VW Laney King wants so bad."

"That's my sister's car," Abigail said, pointing at me.

"I thought so," Marvin said. His gaze slowly shifted to me. "I saw you getting out of it this afternoon. Louisiana plates."

"Yes, sir."

"Are you ladies here on vacation?"

"Yes, sir," Abigail answered.

And, at the exact same time, I said. "No, sir." There was a brief pause. "Sort of," I amended.

"We rented an apartment above the jewelry store. The lease is month-to-month. Abigail's got college in the fall. She'll be headed back to Louisiana in August for that. I might go home then, and I might not. I haven't decided. I heard you mention the job at the hardware store," I added, looking at Daniel.

"Do you want to get a *job*?" Abigail asked, sounding flabbergasted.

"I'm thinking about it," I said. "I've worked at a pharmacy for five years," I added, looking at Daniel. "I can work as a cashier. I worked the cash register and did all sorts of other things at the pharmacy."

"I thought you *still worked* at the pharmacy," Abigail said.

It was the first time I had mentioned getting a job in Galveston, so it didn't surprise me that Abigail was shocked.

"I haven't decided what I'm going to do with my life quite yet," I said, smiling and shrugging at Marvin Jones.

He smiled back at me. "Well, that's all right, young lady... what's your name?"

"Tess Cohen. Tess and Abigail."

"Tess and Abigail Cohen. All right, well, it's nice to meet you two. I guess you'll be staying on Bank Street for at least a month or two."

"Yes, sir," I said.

"My name is Marvin Jones." He put his hand, stiff with arthritis, to his chest. "I own the building next door. Bank Street Boxing. I live upstairs, ever since my wife passed away, so you'll see me around quite a bit."

I wanted to say I was sorry about his wife, but the words got stuck in my throat. "It's nice to meet you," was what I said instead.

"And this boy with the busted-up nose is Daniel King. I'm sure you figured out, by the name, that his family owns the hardware store across the street."

"I was putting that together," I said. I glanced at Daniel. "What position are you looking to hire?"

"Alice was a cashier," Daniel said. "But she was like ninety years old," he added. "You might want to get a job... down at the seawall... or somewhere there's more going on."

I nodded and gave him a little shrug. "I still might want to come by your store though. I'm used to living in a small town."

"You should come by," Daniel said. "Both of you should. I work there. We could hang out sometime."

"That sounds good," I said, nodding. I glanced at Abigail who was nodding also.

"What about tonight?" Daniel asked. "I'm going to a little party at my friend Eddie's house if you want to come."

I saw Abigail look at the door and smile reluctantly, and I glanced that way to find Derek and John had come into the diner. I knew they were going to walk straight up to us.

"We can't tonight," I said to Daniel. "We met these guys earlier and already said we would... drive around with them."

Chapter 6

Billy Castro

Billy did not set an alarm before he went to bed that night. He thought about Marvin Jones and his offer of a boxing lesson, but he talked himself out of going.

In spite of going to sleep late, he woke up at 8am and couldn't go back to sleep. He went back and forth about it, but he ultimately decided to go to the boxing gym. He didn't have anything else to do at nine in the morning, and he had nothing to lose by going.

He parked on Bank Street, right in front of the gym. He could see the front of the hardware store in the rearview mirror of his Mustang. He was a few minutes early so he wasn't in a hurry to get into the gym.

He recognized the people standing in front of the hardware store. It was Daniel King and he was talking to the two girls who sat next to them at the diner last night. They looked alike, but he could tell them apart.

The one with the darker hair kept glancing at his car. She was the one who had been wearing red pants the night before. Today, she had on blue knee-length shorts and a ruffled blouse. She was nothing like the girls he normally went out with. She was proper, innocent, pure. She was talking to the others, but she had looked at his car several times since he pulled up. She had stared at him at the diner the night before, too.

Billy got out of his car and closed the door. He brought a bag with a change of clothes and a pair of tennis shoes in case his jeans and boots didn't cut it in the boxing ring. He had a small duffle bag, and he held it in his hand rather than strapping it over his shoulder on his way inside.

He glanced at the hardware store on his way into the gym, and all three of the people standing outside were looking at him. He didn't care about anyone but the girl on the left. He stared at her and her alone until he turned to walk into the gym.

"I knew you'd come," was the first thing out of Marvin's mouth when Billy walked through the door. "What's in your bag?" he added.

"What should be?" Billy asked.

"Don't answer a question with a question."

"I really want to know, though. What should I have with me?"

"Shorts, gloves, hand wraps or tape. Some proper boxing shoes, eventually, but I know you don't have any of that yet. I have some equipment here. All you need for today is a pair of shorts and some shoes that aren't those."

"Good, because I have none of that other stuff. I brought a pair of shorts and some sneakers, but they're not boxing shoes."

"Sneakers would work, but I can get you a pair of my shoes for today," Marvin said. "Size eleven."

"That'll be fine," Billy said with a nod.

"We'll work in the ring. Coach Lambert is coaching a few guys on the bags, so I'll take you over here and work with you myself."

Billy followed Marvin to the locker room, where he changed into his shorts and laced up his borrowed boxing shoes. The whole place, the whole process, it was all foreign to Billy. But Marvin had done all of it so many times, that he quickly and efficiently walked Billy through every step.

He wrapped Billy's hands with a strip of fabric for support. Billy made a fist and then flexed his hand, smiling at the feel of the wrap. He had never wrapped his hands like that before, and it felt nice. It felt natural. Marvin loaned Billy a pair of boxing gloves, and they made their way to the ring.

The next hour was a non-stop whirlwind of information. Billy had a fresh headwound, and Marvin was sensitive to it being there, but he walked Billy through different punches and stances and boxing principals for a full hour. Billy was competitive and strong-willed, and he was intensely focused on Marvin the whole time.

"Easy, Billy. Easy ones. Nice and easy," Marvin said as they ran through a sequence of punches.

Jab, jab, hook.

Jab, jab, hook.

Jab, jab, hook.

"Let me see jab, cross, hook to the body, and I'm not looking for power, Billy. I just want to see your form. Take it real slow. Easy."

Marvin caught the three punches he asked for. "*Easy* Billy," he said, smiling as Billy performed the combination.

"That *was* easy," Billy insisted. "I was going at about ten percent. How much easier do you want me to go?"

"No, I meant your name. Your nickname. Your fight name. You're Easy Billy Castro."

"I didn't ask for a nickname," Billy said, feeling overwhelmed by all the information and trying not to show it.

"I don't know how many times I said 'easy, Billy' during that practice," Marvin said, shaking his head and wearing a laidback smile.

"I counted three in the last, like, two minutes." Marvin's assistant coach, Dizzy Lambert, chimed in from a few feet away. "I kept looking up there, thinking he was killin' you or something."

"No, but he was gonna kill himself if he didn't slow down. This boy has a two-inch cut on his head, and he's coming in here, wanting to throw a punch like nothing's bothering him."

Marvin reached up and gently slapped the side of Billy's shoulder. "That's all for today, Easy Billy.

64

We'll take it slow while you have that bump on your head. Get changed and come see me in my office."

Billy nodded at Marvin before he started taking off the borrowed gloves. Marvin ducked beneath the ropes and stepped down from the ring using a small set of stairs at the corner.

Billy made his way to the locker room where he changed into his jeans and boots. He made a stack of Marvin's things. He started to leave them on the bench in the locker room. He was going to leave the gym without going to Marvin's office, but he picked up the things and tucked them under his arm.

"Coach's office is right over there."

Billy turned to find Dizzy Lambert was talking to him. Billy had long ago developed an aversion to people in authority, and he almost walked straight out of the gym so Dizzy didn't have the satisfaction of thinking he told Billy what to do. He sucked it up and nodded at Dizzy before he walked into Marvin's office, since he was planning on doing that anyway.

"Come on in," Marvin said, waving Billy inside.

Billy had been in a coach's office before. He played football in high school, and Marvin's office was set up much like Billy's football coach. It was a small, square room with a desk, two chairs, a filing cabinet, and shelves. It was a little messy with papers, knickknacks, trophies, and all sorts of sports memorabilia spread out and hanging on the wall.

Billy set the borrowed items down on the nearby shelf. Marvin motioned for Billy to sit in the chair on the opposite side of his desk, and Billy did as the man asked, sitting on the edge of the chair like he didn't plan on staying.

"I'd like you to be comfortable, Billy."

"I am," Billy said.

"I'd like you to start getting comfortable around me and around this gym. I'd love to see you in here regularly. I'd love to coach you."

"I guess people pay you for that," Billy said, looking around. "I guess that's how you can afford to keep this place open."

"They do," Marvin replied. "The building was given to me, but yes, I do run a business here. I provide a service. I wouldn't expect you to pay me anything, though. Not until we see if we can help each other. You need to give that cut on your head a few weeks, but I'd like to see you and work with you again at that time."

"I could have gone harder today. I don't need to wait three weeks if you're just trying to see what I've got."

Marvin smiled. "Easy, Easy." Marvin hesitated between the two words and said the second one in such a way that he was using it as Billy's first name.

Billy didn't mind the name enough to protest. He figured there were worse nicknames he could have been given.

"Listen, though. I want you to come up here anytime," Marvin said. "Come stop by. I'm here all the time. You can talk to me and meet a few of the athletes—maybe see if you think you might like to try the sport. But I'm gonna make you take a break from boxing with that cut on your head. I can already tell that if you have on gloves, you'll start going hard, so I think it's best to leave the gloves off. Just for a few weeks."

"What's to keep me from going hard other places, when I'm not around here?"

"You are," Marvin said. "You're the only one that can do that. For now, that's your homework. Take care of yourself. Don't injure yourself. Keep yourself healthy, keep yourself out of trouble, and come back and see me again in two or three weeks. I really would love to work with you."

"What do you mean by healthy and out of trouble?" Billy asked.

"For starters, don't do things that can get the sheriff's department called on you."

"I don't. I just run errands for Matty."

"If I hadn't stepped in with that ring, Kenny would have called them on you. He had already figured out that you were the one who had it. He knew your name, and he would have given it to the sheriff."

"That was a one-time thing," Billy said. "That was for cracking me on the head. And threatening me with it."

"Well, maybe you should think about avoiding situations where there's a misunderstanding that can end with you getting cracked on the head."

Billy let out a humorless laugh. "That's just about every situation I'm in," he said.

Marvin gave him a smile that was laced with regret. "Maybe we can work on that. And heal that cut on your head. Take care of yourself. Keep it clean, keep it closed."

"Is there something I should be eating if I'm going to start training?" Billy asked. "Should I change my diet?"

Marvin thought about it for a minute. "I don't know what you eat now, but vegetables. Veggies are always good. Fruit. Fish is good, too. And eggs. You'll be hungry if you start training hard. You'll eat more food than you're used to eating. But we'll get to that."

Billy stood up to leave, but he didn't make it out of the door. He acted like he didn't care, but he wanted Marvin to like him. He was happy that the boxer had taken notice of him, and he wanted to make an impression.

"Do you think I've got talent?" Billy asked even though it wasn't something he'd normally say.

Marvin took off his glasses and set them on his desk. He tilted his head at Billy. "The short answer is yes, son. But that's honestly not worth much. I've seen talented guys fail, and guys with no talent succeed. Talent's only a piece of it. A small piece. So, yes, you're talented, but that's not the main thing I'm looking for. I want the guy that will show up and put the hours in."

"What kind of hours are you talking about?"

"I mean, you could start with like eight or ten a week. But that's for starters. If you end up trying to take it all the way, it'll end up being a lot more than that. Full-time."

"What's all the way?" Billy asked.

"Professional fighting. Big matches."

Billy smiled.

"But there's a lot of work that comes before that," Marvin said. "I'd love to work with you, but you've got a ton of blood, sweat, and tears to look forward to in fighting, son. A lot. Stepping in that ring with thousands of people watching, it's wonderful and it's terrifying at the same time. It takes more than talent to get to that place."

"Is there stuff you can teach me before then? Before the cut heals? If I come around sooner?"

Marvin gave Billy a slow grin. "I'm here to teach whenever you come around, Easy Billy Castro. And I'd be happy to tell you everything I know."

Billy left Bank Street Boxing feeling like he found the missing link. Being in that boxing gym felt natural. Being coached by Marvin Jones felt natural. It was the first time in his life he felt like something really fit.

Billy was inspired by Marvin Jones and his approach to boxing and to life. He felt challenged. He wanted to show Marvin that he had more than just talent. He wanted more of that place, and there was no doubt that he'd be going back.

He wanted to find out where he could get a nice pair of boxing gloves and shoes. He figured he could ask Marvin about it the next time he saw him.

As Billy left, he wondered if tomorrow was included when Marvin said he could come by anytime.

Chapter 7

Tess

"He's coming over here," Abigail whispered. "He's headed this way."

Her face was absolutely stiff, so the words came out funny sounding, but I had been her sister a long time, and I knew how to speak stiff-lipped Abigail. I knew who she was talking about the instant she said 'he' was coming our way. It was Billy.

He had been in the boxing gym for over an hour, and subconsciously, I hoped and planned to be outside when he finished.

Now, it seemed as if my fantasy was coming to pass.

I looked in the direction of the gym and saw Billy. He was crossing the street, looking straight at us, straight at me. Daniel had just gone inside, so it was only Abigail and me who were standing there.

"Have you been standing in this same place the whole time?" Billy asked.

I was not expecting him to speak directly to us, and I certainly wasn't expecting him to say that.

"No. What? No. We left for a while. A long while. Most of the time. We just got back out here a minute ago."

"Tess filled out a job application to work here," Abigail said. "Daniel said his dad would hire her as cashier."

"Are you Tess?" Billy asked, looking at me.

I nodded, my gaze fixed on his. His dark brown eyes were almost black—dark, even in the bright morning sun.

"So, you work here?" Billy asked, glancing up at the hand painted lettering on the window that said King's Hardware.

"Not yet," I said. "I just handed in my job application a couple of minutes ago."

"Daniel's inside, giving it to his dad," Abigail said.

As if he had been summoned, Daniel showed up at the door. He came out a few feet from where we were standing, but we saw it swing open, and Daniel joined us outside.

"I'm hungry," Billy said. He motioned over his shoulder, toward the diner. "I'm going to sit down for some breakfast. Do you want to come over there with me?"

"What?" Daniel asked.

"I wasn't talking to you," Billy said. "I was asking Tess if she wanted to have breakfast with me."

"How do you know Tess?" Daniel asked.

"We just met."

"Not all the way," I said. "You didn't tell me your name." (I knew his name, but I wanted him to say it.)

"Billy," he said.

"I could go for some breakfast with Billy," I said.

"I could too," Abigail said.

"Me too," Daniel added. "I was about to ask if you girls wanted to go there in a little while and get a burger for lunch, anyway."

I made eye contact with Billy. Meeting his eyes came naturally to me. "Do you mind if they come?" I asked.

"If it means you're coming," he said, staring straight at me. I stared back at him. I felt a tingling sensation in my abdomen as a result of his words, his gaze. I could tell he was the type of guy who came out and said what he wanted to say, and quite frankly, I was listening to whatever it was.

"We can all go," I said nodding.

So, the four of us walked across the street to Carson's Diner. Abigail asking to come along, I could understand, but it surprised me that Daniel wanted to come, too, after what happened between them. It surprised me that both of them were okay with it. We seemed like an unlikely combination of people. We sat at a booth, Abigail and me on one side, and Billy and Daniel on the other.

Our waitress, a different lady who introduced herself as Betty, set menus in front of us and told us we could order breakfast or lunch.

Billy ordered breakfast, and I did the same thing even though I had already eaten a fried egg when I woke up that morning. I didn't order a lot—just one egg and some toast. My sister did the same as me, only she made sure Betty would bring grape jelly and butter to go with her toast. Betty said she always did. Daniel ordered a big breakfast like Billy.

"How old are you guys?" I asked as soon as the waitress left the table. It was a preloaded question. I had been thinking of it the whole time Daniel was ordering. I thought of it because Billy ordered like a man, and Daniel ordered like he was trying to order like Billy. I thought maybe he even ordered the exact same thing.

"I was going to ask you that same question," Billy said.

"I'm twenty-three," I said.

"Twenty-five," he said, looking straight at me. "What's your last name?"

"Cohen," I said. "What's yours?"

"Castro. Are you from here?" he asked.

"No. I'm from Louisiana. We are," I corrected, pointing with my thumb to Abigail. "We just moved here a couple of days ago."

"And you already have a job?"

"Not yet."

"She will, though," Daniel said, interrupting. "My dad already said he would hire her after he talks to her old boss at the pharmacy."

Daniel had been the one speaking, but neither Billy nor I looked at him.

"What about you?" I said, clearly looking at Billy.

"I already told you how old I was."

"I wasn't wondering how old you were."

"What were you wondering?" he asked, cracking a smile.

Was he flirting with me?

I tried to remember to breathe.

"Where are you from?" I asked.

"I'm from here. I moved here in middle school."

"Yeah," Daniel said. "You went to high school with Jacob Collier. He's my cousin."

Billy glanced at Daniel and shook his head casually like he didn't know who Jacob Collier was.

"Why'd you move here?" Billy asked.

"Tess didn't want to go to college," Abigail answered. "She wanted to run away to the beach so she could paint pictures of the ocean. But our dad's strict, and he said that was too wild of a plan. So, he settled for having her come to Galveston and stay for a summer. He said it would get it out of her system."

"What do you think?" Billy asked, focusing on me continually. "Do you think it'll be out of your system?'

"It's too soon to tell," I said. "So far, it's a lot more interesting here than it was back home."

"Boy howdy!" my sister said. "It's better here than home *or* Lake Charles. We went cruising on the seawall last night, and I've never seen so many… guys… and girls… people… in my life."

"My dad's paying for our apartment right now," I said. "If I decide to stay past the summer, I'll have to take over my own rent. I'll have to see how all that goes with the job and everything. I'm not sure if I can even afford it. But we're here for two months, at least."

"I'm twenty," Abigail said. "I'm going into my junior year at McNeese."

"College?" Daniel asked. "I've heard of McNeese. What are you studying to be?"

"A teacher," Abigail said. "Little kids, though. I don't like the big kids. They're too mean."

"How old are you, Daniel?" I asked.

"I'll be eighteen in a couple of weeks."

"I thought you *were* eighteen," Billy said. "How'd you get into that card game?"

"Eddie's got a friend that he works with at the service station who knows Matty. I'll be eighteen in a couple of weeks, anyway, so it's no big deal. I've been there with him like five times already."

"It is a big deal to owe Matty that much money," Billy said. "Especially money you don't have. What would you have done if Marvin Jones wouldn't have taken care of it?"

"I would have had to go to my dad, I guess," Daniel said. "And Coach Jones knew I really didn't want to do that. I'm joining the Army soon, and I don't want to leave with him mad at me or disappointed in me."

"I hope you're planning on paying Marvin back," Billy said, pulling back to look at Daniel who was sitting on the same side of the booth.

"I am. I wouldn't let him pay you and not pay him back. He's my coach. I've been boxing with him for over a year—ever since he moved in across the street."

"Are *you* boxing with him now?" I asked. The guys both looked at me, but I was only making eye contact with Billy.

"Me? Yeah."

"You are?" Daniel asked, turning and looking at Billy again. "What happened? What'd he say?"

"I just talked to him," Billy said.

"Did you work with him? Was Dizzy there? Did you hit the bag?"

"We did a little work in the ring, but not much. He wouldn't let me swing hard or anything. Because of my head."

"What'd he say to you?" Daniel said.

"That he wanted me to come back."

"He did? When?"

"Anytime. He doesn't want me to do anything physical just yet—not until my cut heals."

77

Daniel let out a little laugh like that was asking the impossible of someone like Billy. "You didn't tell him you have to get back to work, bustin' skulls."

Daniel was big for his age, but he was younger, more innocent than Billy. He was physically as big as Billy was, but he was like a giddy teenager around the older guy. Billy had come into his life to deliver a threatening message, and yet Daniel seemed to be a fan.

"That's exciting," I said, changing the conversation from busting skulls. I looked straight at Billy. "Do you think you'll get into it? Boxing at that gym?"

"It's hard to say right now, but yeah, I feel like I want to."

"That's amazing," Daniel said. "I can't believe you actually showed up." He smiled and started doing some tiny boxing moves with his fists clinched over the table, blocking his own face. "You're gonna love it. If I wasn't joining the Army, I'd stay home and be a fighter. Coach Jones had ten guys become Golden Gloves champs over the years. Some of them went pro. He's one of the best, and he's right here on Bank Street. A lot of people go over there. Even people who aren't going pro. There are old guys, and even kids learning to box. Even the sheriff goes over there. You want to go pro?" Daniel asked Billy with wide eyed excitement. "Did Coach Jones say he thought you could? He told me I could one day, if I worked at it. He said I have heart. I've got guts. I just need about fifty more pounds."

Daniel was right. He was skinny for a boxer.

He continued to shadowbox lightly, proving his confidence. "If you stick with it for a couple of years, Coach will give you a nickname and a pair of silk shorts with your name on them. And then, you'll wake up ten years down the road with a boxing title and a whole mountain of money." Daniel looked at Abigail and me. "This is assuming you work at it every day," he clarified. "Coach Marvin said you can't go pro without total commitment."

"I got the nickname already," Billy said. "I guess all I need is a pair of silk shorts, and the mountain of money."

"What do you mean you have a nickname?" Daniel said, getting serious as he pulled back to regard Billy. "You can't just tell them a nickname. I'm talking about a fight name. It's different than a nickname. That's not something you give yourself. Coach has to give it to you. It's, like, an official thing. You have to work with him for a long time."

Billy pointed over his shoulder toward Marvin's gym. "He told me some kind of nickname just now."

"Who did? Coach?"

"Marvin, yes," Billy said.

"I don't think so," Daniel said, shaking his head. "I'm not going pro, but I still want a nickname. I've asked Coach Dizzy to talk to Coach Jones about giving me one, but nothing so far. I want to have one before I go off to the Army so I can tell those guys what it is."

"You want a nickname? Why can't you just give yourself one?" Billy asked, shrugging. "No one in the Army would ever know the difference."

"I'd know the difference," Daniel said.

Betty came and set our plates in front of us as we were talking. She said something about leaving extra butter and jelly, and we thanked her.

"What did Coach say?" Daniel asked, still thinking about everything. "When he gave you a nickname? Was it just *Billy*? Are you talking about Billy being short for William?"

"No, he gave me some other name."

"What was it?" Daniel asked, with a disbelieving expression.

"Easy. He said *Easy Billy* or whatever. I don't know if that's the kind of name you were talking about, but that was what he called me."

We all began eating.

"Easy Billy?" Daniel said around a mouth full of food. "What made him call you that?"

"He was telling me to go easy because of my cut."

"Oh, no, that's not your fight name, then. He was just probably messing around."

"It doesn't matter," Billy said with a shrug. "I don't really care about the nickname or the silk shorts. But I will take the mountain of money."

Chapter 8

Abigail and I sat there and ate breakfast with Billy Castro and Daniel King. They both grew up here in Galveston, and they each saw a couple of people they recognized. Our table had a few different visitors while we ate.

The guys didn't know each other before this, so all four of us made small talk. They asked me questions about art, and I told them that I had been practicing for a few months at home, but basically, I was just getting started. They asked about our hometown, and we asked about Galveston.

Daniel talked about boxing, and Billy seemed really interested in learning. He asked questions, and Daniel recounted stories about things he had heard in the gym. They had a big brother-little brother thing going on, and I could tell Daniel was excited that he had information Billy wanted.

We ate together, but the diner was busy, so we paid our tabs and left once we were finished. We all paid separately. It was the most logical thing to do. Billy did look at me more and longer than he looked at my sister, though. He and I had shared several long moments of eye contact while Daniel talked. My heart had raced in those moments. I wanted to get to know Billy Castro. I wanted to paint a picture of him. He was the kind of guy I could easily have a crush on. And maybe I already did.

The four of us walked out of the diner together. Billy's Mustang was parked on the same side of the street as the diner, so we walked that way. It was a dark gold color, like sparkling honey. It was like new, and he kept it clean. I had thoroughly checked it out earlier when he had first pulled up.

"Come hang out with me, Tess," he said, turning to me as we approached his car.

Goodness. Honestly. My name being said by Billy. It made my knees weak.

"And do what?" I asked, even though I'd just about do anything with him.

He shrugged. "I don't know. I was going home if you want to come. My roommates are probably there, so you don't have to worry about us being alone."

"I should go, too, though," Abigail said.

I knew her well enough to know that the idea of Billy's roommates seemed promising.

Billy glanced at my sister. "Do you two go everywhere together or something?"

"No, not back at home," I said. "But at the same time, I don't know about leaving her here just yet." I gestured down the street at our apartment building.

"I'm fine," Abigail insisted.

"Yeah, she's fine," Daniel said.

"It's *you* I was worried about," Abigail added.

"I want to go," I said.

Billy grinned when I said it. "I don't mind if your sister comes," he said. "If it makes you more comfortable."

I glanced at Abigail who gave me a very restrained but pleading expression.

"I'd like for us both to go, if you don't mind," I said.

Billy nodded as if it was fine by him.

"Bye Daniel!" Abigail said. "See ya around."

"Yeah, see ya around," Daniel agreed. "I'll ask my dad what he says about your application," he added, talking to me.

"Okay, thanks," I said as I walked the last few feet to Billy's car.

Daniel hesitated, looking for traffic before crossing the street to go back to the hardware store.

"Will I see you around at the gym?" he asked, looking at Billy before he crossed.

"Yeah, I'll be there," Billy said.

Daniel made an excited expression and gesture with his arm before taking off to cross the street.

I opened the passenger's door. The front seat was a bucket seat, so I reached in, shifted the seat forward, and stood back so my sister could climb into the back. She didn't hesitate to oblige. She had seen the way Billy and I were looking at each other. She knew I had been the one invited to go with him.

I was glad she was with me, though. It wasn't that I didn't trust Billy or think I couldn't take care of myself, it was that I hated to leave Abigail at the apartment alone. We hadn't met our neighbor in 202 yet, and I wanted to give her a few days to get settled before we started leaving each other completely alone on the block. I figured, if I got a job at the hardware store, it wouldn't matter since I'd be right next door all the time.

"Are you okay?" I asked, whispering to my sister as she moved to get into the car.

"Yeah, why?" she whispered back.

"I'm just making sure. I didn't know if you were disappointed about leaving Daniel."

"What? Daniel? No. I'm not interested in… he's seventeen. Plus, I heard Billy say he had roommates." She smiled and raised her eyebrows. "Of course I'm okay."

I rode in the front seat next to Billy. We were separated by a small console, but he was close to me, and I was hyper aware of him as a man. I often sat next to men at work, or church, or in social situations, but I was never ever aware of them like I was with Billy. Everything about him caused my eyes to linger. Everything I saw caused me to feel this warm burn of attraction, the kind where I felt like I might cry if I couldn't find a way to be next to him. His shoulder, his arm, his hands, his leg— everything. Everything my eyes fell onto was good. It was all attractive to me.

Honestly, I wanted to paint him. I couldn't wait until I was a good enough artist to paint him the way I saw in my head. The casual way he sat caused certain shadows in his t-shirt, and I wished I could pull out a sketch pad and take a shot at drawing him right then.

"I moved to Galveston when I was thirteen," Billy said. "It was just my mom and me, but she died when I was sixteen. I've been on my own since then. I live in a big house with four other roommates. All of us just rent our bedrooms, but everybody thinks of it as my house since I've been there the longest. The real owner lives next door."

"Your landlord?" I said.

"Yeah, Matty."

"Oh, the one who's your boss?" I asked.

"Yeah."

"What do you do for him?"

"I work part-time doing some construction, but most of the time, he has me doing errands. Personal favors. He treats me good, and my room is cheap. That's how I was able to pay cash for my car."

"Tess paid cash for her car, too," Abigail said. "By working at the pharmacy."

We had already talked about my Beetle at the restaurant so Billy knew what I drove. He glanced at me when Abigail said I paid for it. One corner of his mouth rose in an approving grin.

I could not get enough of his smile. I shrunk down in my seat, feeling shy about all the feelings I was having.

"What do your roommates do?" Abigail asked.

"Different things. Two of them work together at the hospital. Hank's in college, and Albert likes to do as little as possible. He surfs as much as he can and he works at a restaurant as little as he can. He's got a squirrel for a pet. It's in his room. It rides in his pocket sometimes."

"You're kidding," I said. "Hank and Albert?"

Billy nodded.

"And who are the two who work at a hospital?"

"Cricket and Annabeth. They both work at the same hospital. They're nurses. They work the same shift and always hang out together."

"Are they... women?" I asked. I was so surprised that he would have women roommates that I had gotten stuck on their names and not heard much of what else he had said.

Billy let out a little laugh at my confusion. "Yes."

"Oh, you live with women," I said. I glanced over my shoulder at my sister. It was the first time I doubted myself for going to his house with him.

"It's nineteen-sixty-eight," Billy said. "A guy and girl can live under the same roof and be roommates. They're great tenants. I wasn't going to turn them down just because they're women. If anything, the place is better with them around."

"Have you ever kissed one of them?" Abigail asked.

"Abigail!" I said, turning to face my sister. But secretly, I liked that she was asking.

"I actually have," Billy answered, causing me to experience instant nausea. "But it was a long time ago. Before she ever moved in. We went to the same high school. Nothing's happened since she moved in. She has a boyfriend. You might meet them both. They were at the house when I left this morning."

I was unjustifiably jealous.

I wished Billy had never kissed anyone in his whole life.

I was fuming, and I tilted the side window to let the wind hit me as we drove.

We parked in a driveway, and I looked up at the house that was closest to us, which was blue with white trim. It was a huge, Victorian style wooden home, like most of the others in this area. It was a good color next to his amber colored car.

I tried to think about paint colors. I tried not to think about his female roommates or the fact that I was jealous of them. I made an effort to *not* care about Billy. I would think of this visit as having fun and getting to know new people in Galveston. There was no need to latch onto the first guy who caught my eye. Surely, there had to be some wonderful, decent, available gentleman who didn't beat people up for a living or live with other women.

But in spite of my best efforts to not fall for Billy, I could feel myself doing just that. It was extremely easy to have a crush on him. Physically, he was everything I liked in a man. He had dark hair and eyes, and a wide smile that was confident and laidback.

Abigail and I spent a few hours at his house. It was a lot of fun. His room was upstairs, and it had a little wooden balcony. It didn't have a table and chairs, but we stood out there and looked out at all the colorful homes. Billy played records in his room, and Abigail and I went back and forth from the balcony to sitting on the floor with him. A few times, one of his roommates would come in and talk for a minute, but mostly, it was just the three of us.

I was intrigued by his personality. It wasn't just that he didn't care about impressing me. Billy didn't care about impressing anyone. He was quiet, but when he needed to speak, he was direct and honest. He was funny, but in a serious way. He didn't laugh a lot but he came up with witty responses that made other people laugh.

Billy showed me some new music. He liked rhythm and blues, and several of the artists and bands he played for us were new to me. Abigail knew I was interested in him, and she began asking him questions I would be too shy to ask.

Billy was honest, but he was also a little mysterious. Both of his parents had died, but otherwise he gave very few details of his childhood. As far as I could tell, he had no siblings.

I liked him so much. I could feel myself wanting to gain his approval. I sat up straight around him and tried my best not to say anything I'd regret.

We saw Matty outside when we were leaving for the beach a few hours later. He and Billy had a somewhat awkward encounter where they discussed Kenny's ring. Apparently, someone Kenny knew had told Matty about it before Marvin got the ring back.

Matty didn't seem thrilled about the whole situation, and he also seemed surprised that Billy would want to meet up with Marvin Jones and maybe even start boxing with him. Billy was open and honest with all of the information—the ring, Marvin, and boxing, but Matty didn't seem too happy about any of it.

Maybe that was just how Matty was... not excitable. He acknowledged Abigail and me briefly, but he went right back to talking to Billy. It ended with Billy telling him we were going to the beach and that he'd see him later.

Chapter 9

I was glad I had asked Billy for a piece of paper and a pencil before we left his house because I had the perfect opportunity to sketch a scene while we were out that afternoon.

I definitely needed to get that job at the hardware store. This town was just too picturesque. I was going to need supplies—countless canvases and definitely more colors of paint.

I sketched the scene with Billy and his car on the seafront, situated just right. I put thought into the way everything was positioned, even asking him to park the car in a specific location and facing a certain direction. I took a half-hour to sketch it, using shapes and making detailed notes for myself about colors and shading and general feeling I wanted to remember. There was a little girl with a kite on the beach in the background, and I smiled as I drew her, thinking I couldn't make this stuff up if I tried.

Billy was going to be the star of the painting, though—him and the casual way he sat next to his car, watching people, waiting for me to finish my drawing.

Abigail was off talking to guys. She told me she'd stay close and be back in an hour, which was fine by Billy and me. I folded up the reference drawing and put it in the back pocket of my shorts when I was done with it.

We hung out at the beach during the late afternoon. Billy saw about ten different people he knew. Most of them he just waved at, but a few he spoke to, and a couple he introduced to me. Abigail checked in with me, but mainly she walked a big circle around us, checking things out and talking to people.

Later in the afternoon, she met a group of people she connected with, and she ended up eating dinner with them, leaving Billy and me on our own for dinner.

We talked continuously. He was excited about boxing, and he repeated several of the things his coach had said to him during their meeting. Marvin Jones seemed like a wise man. Billy told me several things he said about life—things Billy hadn't thought of before or that changed his perspective.

Billy and I got along like we had known each other our whole lives. Our conversation was natural and easy, and in the moments when I blocked out the romantic tension I felt toward him, I was able to loosen up and be my slightly goofy self who, like my sister, wasn't afraid to ask him any question.

I'd tell myself to treat Billy like a new friend I'm getting to know, and that would be all good and well for a few minutes, but then I'd catch sight of his mouth, or his hand would move just the right way. Pretty much any time I looked at him, I would lose track of keeping distance and slip into having a huge crush. The moments when I could get away with not looking at him were the best. That was when I had the most self-control.

We spent a full hour just talking to each other while staring out at the gulf. Our conversation continued for a long time while we weren't looking at each other at all. That made it much easier for me. It was hard enough hearing his voice and having him next to me, but not looking helped a lot.

It was well after dinnertime and the sun had just set when Abigail came to meet us at the boardwalk again. The last time she came by with friends, but this time, she was alone.

We all decided to go back to Billy's house for a little while before she and I went home. It was Saturday night, after all, and it was only eight o'clock.

***

We hung out in his living room, and at any given time, there were between two and eight other people there. Billy was popular, and he seemed like he was their ring leader. He was hanging out with them and having fun, but it came across like he was in charge and his opinion was respected.

We stayed there for over an hour before his roommate, Albert, came home. He was with two other guys, and all of them were handsome beach bum surfer guys, like California boys but a little grittier. I knew Abigail would be smitten, and she was.

They sat around the living room. They were drinking beer, and they offered us some, but Abigail and I passed and so did Billy. I didn't know if he was doing that for our sake or not, but either way, he didn't have any.

I sat on the couch with Abigail, and Billy sat at my feet. Every now and then, his back would come into contact with my leg and remind me of how gut-wrenchingly bad I wanted to be next to him. I begged myself to ignore it and focus on other things.

We talked, laughed, and listened to music with Albert and his friends for what must have been an hour or two before Abigail remembered that Albert had a pet squirrel and asked to go see it.

One of them hit the lights on their way out of the living room, and the big overhead light turned on, shining down brightly on us and causing me to squint. It was dark out, and until now, the only light that had been on was a couple of lamps over by the record player.

Billy was still sitting on the floor near my feet, and I happened to be looking down at him when the light came on. He had dark wavy hair, so it had been hidden from me before, but the flash of light caused me to be able to clearly see the cut on the back of his head.

The light turned off just as soon as it turned on.

"Sorry," Albert said, in his laidback surfer's voice since turning it on had been a mistake.

"Bil-ly!" I said in a slow, strained tone.

He turned to look at me curiously when I said his name like that. "What?"

"Your cut. Your head. I saw your cut just now. My goodness!" I reached out gently and put my hand on his shoulder. "I saw it when the light came on," I added. "How have I not seen that all day? How have you just been walking around with that like it's a normal day?"

Billy slowly licked his lips as he smiled. "One thing it has not been for me, Tess, is a normal day." He had turned and was looking at me when he said that. He was definitely referring to meeting me, spending the day with me. He had to be. Maybe he was talking about his encounter with Marvin, but I doubted it, not with the way he was looking at me, looking at my mouth.

"Tess, come here."

"I am here," I said. I felt fizzy inside, like if a giant would pick me up and shake me just the right way, I might explode into a million electric bits.

"You know what I mean," Billy said. "Come all the way here. Come sit next to me."

I glanced around. I knew we were the only two in the room. I didn't hesitate any further. I listened to him, gently sliding off of the couch. I positioned myself, knees tucked, next to him. He leaned toward me and I leaned toward him, both of us moving slowly until our faces were only an inch apart. I smelled him and felt him. The nearness was breathtaking. My heart pounded. I had never in my entire life been as attracted to a man as I was to Billy Castro. He was unbelievably attractive physically, but there was something more to him. He had a certain maturity that was unexpected for someone his age. He had the confidence and patience of a much older man. I was attracted to him on so many levels. I knew I wanted him from the time Daniel and Marvin were talking about him in the alley. I knew I wanted him before I even saw him. I felt destined to be with Billy, and all those feelings culminated in this moment where I finally got to be close to him.

"Do you feel that?" he whispered.

"Yes," I said even though I wasn't positive I knew what he was talking about.

"My chest feels like it's about to crack in half," he said, staring at me, whispering.

"Mine too," I whispered back. I paused for a second before I added, "I can't believe your head. Are you okay?"

He stared at me. There was a record playing. He told me the name of the artist earlier, but it was someone I'd never heard before. The songs were soulful and sultry, and the sounds seemed to go along with what I was feeling. I wanted to be so close to him, that I felt the urge to turn into liquid and let Billy drink me down. He lifted his hand, slowly putting it to the side of my face. His finger barely touched my cheek, and I tilted my head just a little, leaning into his touch.

"Yes, I'm okay," he said, answering my question. "I'm very okay." He paused, staring at me. "But if it makes you feel sorry for me, I'll say it hurts really bad."

"Does it hurt really bad?" I asked, pulling back a little so I could focus on him. "You've been going all around like nothing's the matter, and you should have been at home, resting."

Billy regarded me seriously for a second before speaking. "I can assure you, Tess, I am exactly where I want to be."

"Does it hurt?" as I asked the question, I lifted my hand and touched the back of his head. I did it low on his hairline because I didn't want to get my hand anywhere near his cut. Billy took a deep breath, closing his eyes like he was concentrating all of his efforts into feeling my touch.

"I'm hardly noticing it right now."

"Because you're thinking about other things?" I asked. I didn't mean for it to, but my voice sounded vulnerable.

"Yeah, I'm thinking about other things."

"Is it me?" I said, innocently, quietly.

He grinned. "Yes," he said. "It is you."

His words made it feel like a stream of hot liquid poured through my body.

"She'll probably be back soon," I whispered, knowing that if we were going to kiss, we should get on with it.

"Your sister's in there with Jimmy, now. We'll have to go in there and get her."

I knew the squirrel's name was Jimmy. We had already talked about that.

"Will she fall in love?" I asked.

"Yeah. And she'll be comfortable back there in Albert's room. Him and Hank share that balcony on the south side of the house. It's nice out there."

"So, I guess it's just us, out here in the living room," I said.

Billy grinned. "I guess it is."

"I had fun with you today," I whispered, nervous and shaking.

"Tess... I... think I... like you."

Billy sounded a little surprised, and that made me smile. "I think I like you too, Billy."

"Are we going to see each other again after this?" he asked.

"I think so, I hope so," I said, tentatively. "I want to. I thought that was up to you."

"How is it up to me?" Billy asked. "I'm the one who doesn't deserve someone like you."

"Don't be silly," I said, pulling back a little. I moved my hand from the back of his neck to the side of his face. I gently touched his jaw.

"You're pure, Tess, and I'm not."

"Are you saying you're going to hurt me?"

"The way I'm feeling right now is that I'd do just about anything to keep from hurting you."

I looked into his dark eyes. My heart ached to be with him.

"That sounds like enough to go on," I said.

Billy leaned in and slowly put his mouth on mine. His touch was so gentle that we barely made contact.

"You're... amazing," he whispered as he pulled back. His breath smelled like the hard candy he had eaten from the roll on the coffee table a few minutes before. He kissed my cheek. "Terrific." He leaned to the side and kissed my other cheek. "Beautiful." He kissed my mouth gently, letting his lips linger on mine for a few long, heart-stopping seconds before pulling back. "Exquisite," he whispered.

"You know some fancy words," I said, trying to seem casual, like I wasn't about to lose my mind with desire.

"I'm not trying to sound smart," he said. "It's just that with you, no other words will do. I had to think of the fanciest ones I knew."

"I'm happy we met," I said, smiling.

I was breathless when I said it, and it was obvious that *happy we met* was an understatement. Billy pulled me to him, catching me up, leaning in and covering me with his kiss. My mouth clung to his. It was like we were experiencing a gravitational pull. I was definitely pulled to Billy. My body went willingly to him. He received me gently, wrapping me up in his arms, supporting me, holding me, kissing me. He let his mouth mold to mine, our lips softening and fitting together.

He pulled back one time before leaning in and kissing me again. For the next minute or so, he gave me slow, warm, wet, perfect, open-mouthed kisses.

Billy could have kissed me deeper. I would have let him. But he was using restraint. I could feel palpable tension coming off of him as he held me and kissed me. His breathing was irregular and he seemed shaken with the effort to take things slow. I wanted so badly to give him permission to kiss me more, beg him to do it. But I knew I couldn't.

Billy's mouth. It was warm and soft, and I loved the way it moved and the way it tasted. It touched mine continually. He would try to stop and then decide to kiss me again.

I honestly didn't know these types of feelings were possible.

I was in a different world when Billy kissed me, and I wasn't looking forward to leaving.

Chapter 10

Two weeks later

Billy and I had seen each other quite a bit lately. Some days, we'd only get to talk for an hour or so, but there were several days during those weeks where we spent the entire day together, from early morning until well into the night. My sister liked to come along for part of the time when we spent a day like that. She was smitten with Albert, and she liked to hang out at Billy's house any opportunity she got.

Billy and I hadn't talked about becoming an item yet, but we were compatible and we both seemed to be having a good time getting to know each other. The truth was that I had a gigantic crush on him, but I got the impression that he wasn't really the girlfriend type. Everyone in his life seemed surprised that I was around as much as I was.

I got that job at the hardware store, and I made quite a bit of time to hang out with my sister and to paint, but I saw Billy anytime I wasn't doing those other things.

He had been coming to the boxing gym every day. I got to know his schedule, and we would make a point of running into each other when he was on his way out of the gym.

We had kissed a few times since that first night, but it was never in front of my sister or anyone else. We came across as friends even though I really liked him and wanted him to be my boyfriend.

I knew it was a good idea to take things slowly, and Billy seemed to be guiding things that way, so I went along with it. It was for this reason that didn't feel bad when I made other plans that Friday night.

Billy had to do something for work with Matty, so I originally thought I would stay home and paint. It was the weekend, however, and my sister's pestering got the better of me, so I ended up going out with Abigail and her friends.

We parked at a busy drive-in diner on Seawall Boulevard, in a row of other cars. One of Abigail's friends had a convertible, and Abigail and I sat on the top of the back seat, talking to people in nearby cars while Abigail's friends, three guys and a girl, stood in a group between us and another car.

They called her Abby. No one back home or in Lake Charles ever called her that. Daniel King had started the nickname, actually. She liked it, though, and she now introduced herself that way to new friends she made in Galveston.

Carl, one of the guys in our group, came up to the side of the car to show us a magic trick. He showed us a coin and then he reached toward me and pulled it out from behind my ear. It was a trick my dad had been pulling on me since I was three years old, but Carl was serious and thought I would react.

He was sweet, and he was trying to impress Evelyn, the other girl in their group, so I smiled and acted amazed by his trick.

I had just finished doing this kind favor for Carl when I glanced at the street in front of us. It was past dinner time, and the sun was going down. But there were lights, and I could clearly see the honey-brown Ford Mustang cruising down the street in front of us.

It took a second for my eyes to travel to the window of the car so that I could see who was driving. By the time I caught sight of him, he was already driving past me. Billy. His window was down and he was looking straight at me. We held eye contact for a few seconds. I wondered what he had seen, how long he had been watching. He didn't look happy. My stomach dropped. I definitely looked guiltier than I was in this situation. *But did he even care if I was flirting with another guy? Maybe he was jealous, and maybe he wasn't.* I couldn't tell from his straight-faced expression.

Either way, my heart was pounding. I felt like I wanted to run out into the street and catch Billy so that I could explain. But just like that, he was gone. He had to turn to face the street as he drove. He looked away from me, and then his car got lost in the traffic.

It hit me, only after he drove off, that he had other people in the car with him. There was no way he could be jealous of me if he was out with other people. I felt myself wondering if they were guys or girls. I felt all sorts of jealous feelings. I wondered when I'd see him again.

I knew he usually went to the gym on Saturday mornings while I worked at the hardware store, and we would meet up on Bank Street afterward. I was already thinking about the next time I'd see him. I thought maybe he would call me later tonight. I hoped that would happen.

It didn't.

I didn't hear from Billy at all that evening.

I painted to try to get my mind off of him, but I had a hard time. I kept remembering the way he was looking at me as he drove past.

***

I was glad I had to work the following morning because it got my mind off him.

I had been painting so much, and canvases were so expensive, that I had taken to making my own. It was Mr. King's idea. I was talking about the cost of canvases one day, and he said I should build my own. He called a friend who knew how to do it, and so far, I had made four of them. They weren't quite up to par with the ones I purchased pre-made, but I thought stretching canvas to just the right tautness might be the kind of thing I would get better and better at with practice.

Mr. King had ordered me some thicker canvas, and it had come in. It was waiting for me at the register when I got to work. I was happy to have that distraction, because otherwise I'd be thinking about

Billy non-stop. I'd be thinking about the fact that it was 9am and his car wasn't parked in front of Marvin's gym.

Saturday was busy at the hardware store. I worked from 8 to 12, which were the busiest hours. The manager and a few others always got to the store and opened up at 7am, and someone always stayed till 3, but my shift was 8 to 12.

The Kings came in at 9am. Just like clockwork, Daniel's parents walked into the front door. I was helping a customer find something, and I got a good view of them through the window as they came in.

Mrs. King had clearly been crying. She was always the put-together type, smiling and walking like a lady, but today she was wiping at her eyes and scowling, so I knew something had upset her.

I showed the customer to the screw hooks he was looking for and then went around the back way to my register.

"It's that Billy boy," she complained. "Ever since Marvin got him to join that gym, Daniel's been *Billy this* and *Billy that*. I'm calling Marvin and saying something to him. I knew that boy would lead to trouble. Daniel had a busted nose the first day he showed up, and I heard him listening to some kind of rock music the other day that sounded like somebody was just going crazy on the guitar."

"Daniel makes his own decisions," Nathaniel said.

"Yeah, but we should have a say in who influences him," she said. "And it shouldn't be that Billy guy. I mean, really, Nathaniel, what's he want with Daniel?"

"He'll be eighteen in a few days, Nancy. He's joining the Army. He's got a lot on his mind. He's just blowing off a little steam with his friends."

"He was still drunk just now!" she said. "How are you still drunk in the morning? He was sleeping in my flowerbed, for goodness sake."

"I know he was, Nancy. I saw him. I'm the one who helped him in. I'm not saying he's… hello, Tess, how are you, sweetheart?" Mr. King paused to greet me when they walked past.

"Fine," I said.

"You didn't happen to see Daniel last night, did you?"

"No, sir," I answered.

"I see you talking to that Billy Castro," Nancy said.

"Yes, ma'am."

"Does he ever try to influence you to go out drinking?" She stared at me with an intense expression.

"No, ma'am," I said, feeling stunned by the direct question. She was obviously shaken. "Why? Is everything okay?"

"Daniel got into some trouble last night," Nathaniel said.

"He's lucky he didn't get himself killed," Nancy said, sounding more frantic than her husband. "It's no telling how he got himself home."

"Are you sure he'd been drinking?" I asked trying to smooth things over.

"He smelled like a liquor store," Nathaniel said.

And at the same time, Nancy King said, "He was still drunk this morning. He slept in my daylilies!"

She was not happy. Her face was red and her eye makeup had smeared. I felt bad. I wanted to take up for Billy, but I didn't know how to. It made my stomach hurt to think of Daniel getting into trouble with Billy.

I knew they had been getting to know each other at Marvin's gym, but I had no idea they were together last night. I certainly didn't know they went out drinking. It made my heart ache to hear them say such harsh things about Billy.

I didn't know what to say, so I went about my business, working the register and helping customers like always. I should've been excited about my new canvas, but all I could think of was Billy now.

I wondered what happened the night before. I wondered where he was now and when I would talk to or see him again. I kept thinking he was mad at me for what he saw at the drive-in. I kept wishing I could talk to him and set things straight.

***

It was 10:30am when his car finally parked in front of Bank Street Boxing. I could clearly see him from where I was standing, and I watched as he got out of his car and went inside the gym. He was late, and he wore a straight face when he headed inside. He wasn't the type of man who would just walk around with a goofy smile on his face for no reason, but he also used to spare me a glance on his way into the gym, and today he didn't. He didn't even look my way. My heart ached.

I got off work at noon, and I was hoping to meet him on Bank Street at 12:30 or so, but I didn't know if that was happening today. I clocked out at 12, and I ran up to my apartment where I freshened up and changed clothes.

Billy always commented on this one powder pink top of mine, so I put it on with some knee-length jean shorts and some sandals. My sister was home, and I asked her to braid a couple of sections in the top part of my hair. I wore the rest of it down over my shoulders. I got dressed as quickly as I could so that I wouldn't miss Billy when he came out of the gym.

I was relieved to see that his car was still parked there when I came downstairs. I waited near the door to the apartments for long enough that Laney King, Daniel's little sister, came out of the hardware store to talk to me. She wasn't working. She had a sleepover the night before with a friend from school and she got dropped off at the hardware store afterward. I talked to her while I waited.

It must have been thirty minutes later when Billy finally appeared. I reached out and touched Laney's arm when I saw him.

"I'm going to talk to my friend, okay? I'll see you later."

"Okay," she agreed, easily.

Chapter 11

Billy saw me coming, and he still walked toward his car. Last week and the week before, he came across the street to meet me. I was excited to see him, and my body was all full of anticipation. I figured he might be going to his car to put his bag away, so I jogged across the street to talk to him.

"Hey," I said once I got closer.

"Hey," he said. He opened his car door and tossed his bag into the passenger's seat. He wasn't smiling. He wasn't even looking at me. My heart dropped.

"Whatcha doin'?" I said, trying to sound upbeat. I reached out and touched his arm—just barely, but I did it. Billy stepped back and took a deep breath.

"What's the matter?" I asked.

"Nothing. Marvin, Coach Jones, he just put me through a fff—" Billy made a noise, cutting off. He was about to cuss, but he didn't. "I was running late. I almost didn't come today. And when I did get here, he really tried to kill me. I'm feeling sick from it. I'll probably just go home."

"It's only your second day," I said, feeling protective.

Billy had been spending a lot of time at the gym. He was doing a few light drills and being mentored by Marvin this whole time, but the cut on his head was newly healed, and yesterday was his first day doing a full workout.

"Something must have happened," Billy said. "Coach was upset. He said I shouldn't drink when I'm training, and even when I'm off the clock I'm on the clock and a bunch of other stuff I wasn't ready to hear today. I didn't want to come in the first place. I wanted to sleep-in and skip it altogether. I should have done that."

"I'm sorry it was a hard workout," I said. "Mr. Jones must have talked to Daniel's parents. They were upset this morning. I heard them talking about Daniel coming home in bad shape."

"I don't know what that has to do with me," Billy said.

"They were saying they thought Daniel was with you last night."

He shot me an offended stare. "He *was* with me last night," he said.

"Yeah, well, they were upset."

"About what? He's a grown man. He's going to boot camp and probably to war after that. He was just trying to blow off steam."

"They were saying… you know… about you being an influence, or whatever."

Billy stared at me with that same offended scowl, shaking his head at me. "I'm not Daniel's babysitter. I didn't even see him half the night, anyway. He was hanging out with Albert and all them." Billy was clearly upset. He had been on edge since the moment I came over.

"I was just saying that because it could have been a reason Coach Jones took it hard on you. The Kings were complaining about Daniel. They might have called him." I attempted a smile, wishing we could get back to our normal dynamic. "Anyway, I'm just glad to hear you're upset about your workout," I added. "I was hoping there was no misunderstanding about last night. I was with my sister and her friends."

"Yeah, I saw that," Billy said. "I'm really not worried about it. It needed to happen sooner or later, anyway."

I felt instantly frustrated, flustered, heartbroken. He was being distant. It was like he didn't even want to talk to me. I was mad at Billy for being so aloof after how much we had built our relationship during the last two weeks.

"What needed to happen?" I asked.

"You need to do your own thing, Tess. You'll only be in Galveston for the summer. You need to go off on your own while you're here."

"What does that mean? I thought I *was* doing my thing. Everything I'm doing feels pretty much like *my thing*."

Billy glanced at me. He did this biting motion on his lip like he did every time he was thinking about something. "Look, Tess, it's been fun hanging out and everything, but we both know this is over in a few weeks. It's best we focus on our own things right now. Marvin just wiped the floor with me in there."

I stared at him in disbelief.

Was I being broken up with?

Was that what was happening here?

My heart felt crushed. I experienced an actual crushing sensation, like a heavy weight was bearing down on my chest. Tears sprang to my eyes. There was nothing I could do to hold them back.

"I was with my sister and her friends last night, Billy. What you saw wasn't—"

"It doesn't matter what I saw," he said. "I'm not asking for an explanation."

"Can I please give you one? Can I please talk to you for five minutes before you just drive off?"

Billy glanced around. Mrs. Harper was, no doubt, looking down over the street, and there were others, including Laney, who were curious about Billy and me.

"Would you please just step into my apartment for a minute?" I pleaded. "My sister's up there. We made a big pot of spaghetti this morning to keep in the ice box for a few days. You should come eat some. I thought you would."

Billy touched his stomach instinctually as he looked away. "I'm definitely not hungry after that workout."

"Would you still come up for a second?" I asked. "Let's just talk for a minute before you drive off. I've been waiting for you."

I could tell that Billy was reluctant, but he decided to give in and come with me. He closed the car door and locked it before crossing the street with me. We walked up the stairs and into my apartment where we could finally get a moment alone. My sister was in the kitchen, but she was listening to music and not paying attention to us.

I was so anxious that I started talking the instant we got into the living room. "I have no idea why you're upset. It feels crazy that you won't even let me explain about last night. You won't even look at me."

We were standing in the middle of my living room, and he glanced at me when I said that.

"You don't need to explain," Billy said. "I don't care."

"You don't care about me?" I asked.

"I didn't say that. I said you don't need to explain what you were doing. You should go be with that guy. Or someone else like him. I'm not the right guy for you, Tess. And it's best if we stop spending so much time together."

"Billy, where is this coming from?"

"Tess, eventually I'm not going to be with you. And seeing you with that guy last night made me realize that I should just let you go so you can enjoy your summer and be with someone else."

"I don't want that. I don't want to be with anyone else."

It was an insane conversation to be having with my sister in the next room. I wanted to raise my voice, and I couldn't.

"Well, this isn't going anywhere," he said. "The faster you accept that, the better off you'll be." He paused staring straight at me. "Don't. Don't. Tess, don't cry."

A silent tear fell onto my cheek, and I swiped at it stubbornly with the back of my hand. "I'm not trying to cry," I said, gathering my wits. "I'm just frustrated that you're not giving me a vote in this. If you don't like me, just say it. It's easier that way."

"Fine, I… I… I don't…. I don't like you. I decided that I…" He paused and let out a long sigh. "Tess, I'm not who you think I am. I'm not a normal guy. I'm not going to marry you and have a baby and a house, and all that stuff you want. I'm not that guy. You need to meet somebody good. You don't need to waste time with me."

"Please stop making this about you," I said. "I like you. I want to be with you. I don't think it's a waste of time. If you're going to stop spending time with me then just come out and say you don't want to."

Billy grabbed me by the arms. He had a gentle but firm hold on me. He would have let me go if I would have resisted, but I didn't. I stared at him, begging him with my expression to be reasonable. Our living room was small, and we could hear my sister humming along to her music. I paid no

114

attention to anything but Billy. I could not understand what had happened to flip the switch with him.

"I am not a normal man," he whispered slowly. He took a deep breath and made a contemplative expression as if trying to decide on the right words. "I am a bad man, Tess. I'm bad for you and I'm bad in general."

"Listen, I was thinking about that," I said. "Some of those times where people end up thinking bad things about you, some of that is avoidable. Like with Daniel, you're right, you're not his babysitter and he makes his own choices. But maybe next time, you can just make him sleep at your house instead of in his mom's flowerbed."

Billy opened his mouth like he was about to say something, and then he closed it again, hesitating. "I'm not talking about Daniel right now, Tess. That's really the least of my worries. He can work that out with his parents. I really don't care what they think about me."

"Yes, you do. You're trying to sit here and tell me you're a bad person, and I'm trying to tell you that you don't have to be seen that way. You can change people's perception of you."

"Tess, I don't care what people think. You should know that about me by now." He took his hands off of me and put his palm to his chest. "It's me. I'm not a normal person. There are things you don't know about me. Huge, life-changing things.

Things that would definitely change your mind about me. Just take my word for it. I've lived through things that I don't even talk about. The faster you move on to somebody else, the better off you'll be."

"What if the things you've lived through don't make me feel any different about you?" I asked. "Does that count for anything?"

"It honestly makes this harder," he said. "I just need to not look at you, Tess. If we can just look the other way and leave each other alone, we'll both be… better off."

Billy had been looking downward as he spoke, and I tried to get him to look at me by tilting his face with my fingers. He resisted a little, so I stopped touching him, but he made eye contact with me.

"I don't care what it is, Billy," I said quietly.

Billy took me by the arms again. He took a deep, uneven breath. I could feel the tension radiating off of him. He was restraining himself, but power and emotion emanated off of him. He leaned down and put his mouth near my ear and whispered intently.

"I'm warning you that what I'm about to say will make you hate me. It'll make you scared of me."

"Tell me," I begged, whispering in his ear.

"I killed my father," he said. "I shot and killed my father when I was thirteen years old." He swallowed. His whisper was hoarse. I stayed quiet, assuming he would say something else. "My mom took the blame. She said she had done it in self-defense, and everyone believed her because he used to beat her so bad." Billy paused for another deep breath, but I just stayed still, waiting to hear what else he would say. "My mom never got over it, and three years later, she overdosed on alcohol. This was ten years ago," he added. "And before that, I lived a childhood of straight fear. Living with my father was pure torture. I am not a normal person, Tess. I feel like I'm fifty years old right now. Eighty years old. I'm not capable of having a girlfriend or a wife and kids and all that. There's darkness in me. It has nothing to do with you. You are everything a man could want. It's all I can do not to... I'm having to stop myself from falling... it's not about you, Tess. I'm sorry if you're scared of me now, but I had to make you see why I can't—"

"I'm not scared of you," I said, grabbing onto him when his grip loosened on me. I wasn't looking at him when I said it, but I knew he heard me. He had been whispering near my ear the whole time, and our eyes weren't connected, but we were close. His mouth was near my ear.

He took a long, measured breath when I said I wasn't scared of him, and I reached out and gently wrapped my arms all the way around him. I moved slowly, but once I realized that he was letting me do it, I wrapped my arms around his mid-section, burying my face on his chest, and squeezing him firmly. His arms didn't come around me to hug me back. He felt stiff and rigid, and I didn't realize until a few seconds later that he was crying. He was crying without making a sound. He was crying so hard that his entire stomach and chest were flexed and seized-up with the effort of one long sob. I held him tighter. He was hot to the touch, and he cried in long, almost silent breaths like there was ten years of emotion stored up, and it was seeping out of the cracks all at once. He let out long, wheezing breaths. He cried tightly, in a masculine way like it almost hurt to come out.

I just stood there and held him as securely as I could. After what felt like a full minute, Billy took a deep breath like he was about to speak.

"Please don't tell anyone," he said, finally. "Not even your sister. I shouldn't have told you that just now. I just—"

"I won't," I promised. And I meant it. I pulled back far enough to focus on him, but he glanced away. "Billy, look at me," I said.

He glanced at me, but he had a hard time. He was wearing a serious, almost dazed expression. His eyes met mine, but he seemed disconnected.

"I'm still here," I whispered, staring straight into his watering eyes.

He looked at me for several seconds. "Why?" he whispered.

"Because I still want to be with you," I said, unflinching. "That didn't change after what you said just now."

He was slow to respond and he looked confused and disbelieving, but finally, he said, "How?"

"What do you mean, how?"

"I mean how could you want to stand here and still look at me after what I just said? Did you even hear me?"

I stared into his sad, disbelieving eyes. He was a young man, and he had lived through things I couldn't imagine. I felt no fear or trepidation toward him. I felt only love and empathy. I wanted to help him love himself again.

"I don't think you heard what I said," he said again, still looking confused, unconvinced.

"I did hear you, Billy," I said. I had loosened my grip on him when I pulled back, but I hugged him again, resting my head against his chest and reassuring him. "I heard you, and I'm not scared at all. I don't want you to leave. It makes my heart feel broken when you talk about not spending time with me anymore."

Chapter 12

Billy wrapped his arms loosely around me, tentatively holding me. I had just held him tightly while he let out a stream of unrelenting tears. He had been unable or unwilling to hold me in return until this point, and my heart grew happy when I felt him move to take me into his arms.

He had showered at the gym, and he smelled like soap. I could feel his muscular body, and somewhere in the back of my mind, I knew I was attracted to him. But that wasn't a thought I was having at this moment. Right now, I had to make sure his heart was okay. I continued to hold him, but I leaned back to look at him. I reached up and wiped at his tear-soaked cheek with my thumb.

He had said enough that I knew he had killed his father because he was being abusive. I could see the hurt and distant coldness in his eyes. I wished I had been there to comfort him when he was a child.

"I figure we'll talk more about it and say more about it later, Billy. But for now, can you just know that I want to be with you? Please just know I still want to be next to you after what you said."

"I don't understand how you could," he said. "I don't feel like I'm suited to be with anyone, Tess. Especially someone like you. You deserve everything. You deserve someone normal without a... such a... you deserve someone who's whole."

"No one is whole," I said. "Everybody's imperfect. It's just a matter of whether or not your imperfect fits well with my imperfect."

"I'm pretty sure I have a type of imperfect that doesn't fit with anyone."

"I see that you're pretty sure about that," I said sarcastically, referring to that fact that he was standing there holding me.

Billy just stared at me like he couldn't believe that I was still standing there. He was actually convinced that I would leave after he told me those things. He hadn't imagined himself in this situation. I could tell by his expression that he didn't know what to say to me next.

"Did you think that because of what you did all those years ago that you're just not going to ever have anything lasting? No lasting relationships? No family relationships?"

"I have friendships and stuff," he said. "But no. Not a family or anything. No."

"Well, I'm sorry, but I can't let you do that. I can't let you just, go away from me that easy. I'm too used to having you around me now, and this information doesn't change that… not on my end."

My sister picked that moment to walk from the kitchen to the living room.

"Oh, hey, Billy, I didn't even know you were here. Did you come to see the painting? Tess finished it yesterday. I was looking at it this morning thinking *Billy's going to love this one*. Are you…"

Abigail hesitated once she came more fully into the room. "Are you *crying*?" She sounded confused because Billy was not a crier. She had gotten to know him well enough to know that he was not the type to cry.

"Billy got sick while he was over at boxing," I said. I pulled him to the couch with me, and he followed without hesitation.

"Oh, really?" Abigail asked, looking concerned. "Is it his stomach?"

I nodded.

She had a bowl full of spaghetti and she stopped in her tracks. "I think I'll go eat this in the bedroom, if your stomach's upset," she said.

"You don't have to," Billy said.

"It's fine. I need to go in there and call Evelyn, anyway. She's coming to pick me up in a little while, and I need to figure out what I should wear."

Abigail disappeared into the next room as Billy and I got comfortable on my couch. He sat in the corner, and I curled up next to him, drawing near and assuring him that I didn't feel differently.

"Tell me everything," I said.

"What?"

"If you want to," I corrected. "You don't have to. But I was just thinking... I don't mind hearing more... if you want to talk about it."

Billy took a deep breath. I situated myself where I was facing the back of the couch, facing Billy. I leaned onto his lap and reached up to touch the side of his face. I was looking at him, loving on him, doting over him. I felt like he was owed that after he had been carrying such a heavy weight for so long. I was happy to be the one to help him through it. It was instantly my mission to make Billy know he was capable of redemption. That task felt like a joy to me. I needed to let him know he was capable of living a good life. I had to show him he could do it. I had to show him how. My heart was drawn to Billy now more than ever.

He sighed. I didn't know if he was going to tell me more or not.

"My mom and I took regular beatings when I was a kid. My dad drank a lot, and he got violent a lot, too. I didn't plan on doing it. I didn't think about it before it happened or anything. We fought, and he was taking drugs, so I just couldn't hurt him enough to knock him out. He just kept coming at me. My mom was already too hurt to help me. I was in a bad situation, and I had access to his gun, so I used it. In that moment, I felt like it was him or me. I pointed it at him, and I pulled the trigger. I can't believe I'm even saying that out loud." He paused for a long minute and took a deep breath before continuing. "I haven't said it to anyone since my mom, and even then, it was only once, and she wasn't... I don't know. It all happened so fast. I told her I did it, and she told me to never tell anyone. She had a busted face and bruises all over her body to go with her confession of self-defense, and she didn't serve any jail time. We moved to Galveston to get a fresh start, but she drank herself to death after that. She wasn't much of a mom before that, but afterward, I hardly knew her. I think she might have been scared of me. I don't know if she was or not. Things changed after the thing with my dad, and I was just alone. I have friends, and I come across as fairly normal, but I'm not normal, Tess."

"Why do you feel the need to keep warning me about that?"

"Because I don't expect you to continue seeing me," he said. "I think once all this sets in, you'll want to reconsider. And I won't blame you for it."

"Yeah, but what if I don't?" I asked. "Do I get to be with you? If I can handle who you are, and what you did, and who you really are inside, do I get to be with you?"

Billy gave me a slow smile and let out a breath, and I stretched up, kissing his cheek. I did it three or four times slowly, tasting the salt of his tears.

"Do I?" I asked before kissing him again.

"Yes, Tess. Of course."

"Of course, what?" I asked, feeling dazed by the taste and feel of him.

"Of course, you can be with me. I don't know why you'd want to after knowing what I—"

I kissed his mouth to stop him from talking. "Please don't ever say that again," I said. "Don't say you don't know why I would want to be with you. I can think of a thousand reasons why I want to, Billy.

I'm sorry you had to go through what you went through. I'm not mad, or scared, or judgmental of you. I'm sorry." I kissed the corner of his perfect mouth. "I want to help you heal from all that and move on."

My words must have been too much for Billy because he squinted and rubbed his eyes with his hand, being too manly to cry. I curled up next to him, cuddling against his chest.

"I don't care if you can't make me any promises," I said. "I just want to be next to you right now."

"I want to be next to you right now, too," he said thoughtfully.

I picked up my head and looked at him. He had a few small scars on his face from different things that had happened over the years. He had more on other parts of his body, but I had only seen him without a shirt on a few times, and I hadn't checked out his scars. It was bright enough in the living room that I could clearly see the ones on his face. I appreciated them in a new way now that I knew about his background.

I was raised in a small town by strict parents. It wasn't common for me to sit across a man's lap like I was doing right then. Billy and I didn't usually get this comfortable with each other, either. But today was different. There was a certain level of intimacy to the things we discussed, and sitting across his lap was the minimum of what I felt like doing right then.

Having that thought caused me to experience a wave of desire. I wanted to kiss him so badly that for a few heart-pounding seconds, it was hard to concentrate on anything else.

"You keep staring at me," Billy said.

He had been saying something else, but I tuned in when he accused me of staring.

"Yes, I'm staring at you," I said. "Sorry. I finished that painting last night, but I might have missed something on your face." I reached out and touched the space near the edge of his mouth. "I need a shadow right there." (The truth was that I was thinking more about kissing Billy than shadows and paintings.) It was basically an excuse. I had been blatantly staring at his mouth, and I wasn't sure if he wanted to kiss me right then, so I had to make something up.

"You're studying me pretty hard," he said. I saw his lips move when he spoke because I was, well, still staring at his mouth. He grinned, and I just kept right on staring. *How was I supposed to look away when his mouth looked like that?*

"I'll protect you," I said, staring dazedly at him.

"I'll protect you, too, Tess. I'll never hurt you."

"I know you won't," I said. "I feel safe with you."

"I hope you do," Billy said.

I put my arms around him, hugging him again. "How are you feeling?" I asked. "After the workout."

"What workout?" Billy said.

I smiled and lifted my head to look at him.

"Tess."

"Yeah?"

"I wanted to hit that guy last night."

I laughed because I didn't expect him to say that. "That's my sister's friend. He likes the other girl that was with us. Evelyn. He was showing off for her. He did that *coin behind the ear* trick on me to impress her."

"Oh, poor guy," Billy said. "He almost got misunderstood."

"I know. Next time you see me at the drive-in, just turn around and come pick me up."

"I will," he said.

"Good," I returned. "I dare you."

"You don't have to dare me," Billy said. "I'll do it without a dare. I'll pull a U-ey in the middle of Seawall Boulevard and peel out on my way into the drive-in. I'll cause a big scene."

"No, you wouldn't," I said, grinning.

"I'm not going to if I don't have to. As long as other guys keep their hands off my girl, I won't have to peel out, or punch people, or anything else."

I laughed a little. "Are you jealous over me?"

"Do I have any reason to be?" he asked.

"No."

"Then, no, I'm not." He scanned my face and then smiled. "But nobody better ever touch you, or talk to you, or look at you."

I smiled back since I knew he was kidding around, and he used a finger under my chin to tilt my face up. I took that finger-to-the-chin move as permission. I leaned upward and kissed him gently.

Billy opened his mouth to me instantly. We kissed for a second or two before he readjusted on the couch, sitting up so that he could use his hands to touch the sides of my face. He wrapped one hand around the back of my head and pulled me in, kissing me deeper. I gripped the fabric of his shirt, balling my hands into fists.

Billy tilted his face to the side and the next thing I knew, his tongue was making a gentle intrusion into my mouth. I welcomed it, opening, taking him in, pulling him closer. I was the one who drove the kiss, deepened the kiss. Billy was trying to be gentle like he always was. He was trying to be a gentleman. And that was usually all fine, but today we had grown closer.

As odd as it sounded on a day when I had learned about Billy's past, today was the first day I could see my forever with Billy. I kissed him accordingly. I invited him to kiss me deeply, and he responded, covering me with a scorching, branding kiss. He gave me a possessive, hot, silky, liquid kiss, and I welcomed it. I gripped Billy tightly and moved, maintaining the smooth, rhythmic motion.

Billy gave me that earth-shatteringly deep kiss for several minutes before pulling back. Both of us were breathing heavy when he broke contact. His mouth came down on mine again—two, three, four times—hard kisses. They were the exclamation points on what had been a life changing kiss. I was out-of-it and breathing heavy when he finished kissing me.

"I love you," I said. I touched the side of his face, letting my thumb brush the edge of his mouth to keep him from talking. "You don't need to say it back," I added. "I don't want you to yet, actually. I know you didn't expect me to say it. But I wanted you to know that. I do love you, Billy. I know I do."

Chapter 13

Billy

Another two weeks later

Billy was standing next to a window in Tess and Abigail's living room, looking down over the alley. With the way he was facing, he could see a little piece of 23rd Avenue, and he absentmindedly watched an old man walking down the sidewalk with a cane.

Billy was waiting on Tess. She was in the bedroom getting ready for the walk they would take before he had to come back to Bank Street for an afternoon training session.

It was safe to say that Billy wanted to pursue boxing. He had been at the gym every single day. He was trying hard and working hard, and Marvin just kept pushing and encouraging him.

Marvin had Billy thinking he could make a career out of boxing if he kept going at the rate he was now, and Billy really wanted to. It was the first career choice that seemed natural to him, and Marvin seemed to think he was born to do it.

Billy was thinking about boxing as he watched the man walk slowly down the sidewalk. He couldn't help but listen to Abigail's conversation in the next room. She was in the kitchen, talking on the phone, and Billy could clearly hear her.

"Oh, yes ma'am. That's no problem. My sister has a car, and she can give me a ride to your house. ... Oh, that'll be amazing. Thank you. ... Yes ma'am. All of July. I'm not leaving till the end of the month. ... Yes ma'am. Thank you. ... Okay, see you tomorrow. Thank you. Bye-bye."

Abigail appeared in the living room only seconds after she hung up the phone. "Looks like somebody has a babysitting job," she said.

"A babysitting job?" Billy asked. "That's what that was about? I thought you won a sweepstakes or something. You said 'thank you' too much for a babysitting job. I thought it was something good."

"It *is* something good," Abigail said. "That was Mrs. King's friend. Last time I babysat for her, she gave me *twenty dollars*. They're so rich. And the kids aren't even brats. They're fun to hang out with. And, anyway, Billy, thankfulness is good, even if they weren't paying me twenty dollars. It's nice of me to say 'thank you' to her. You need to say it way more, if you ask me."

"What's that supposed to mean?" he asked.

"You need to thank people more," Abigail said with a shrug. "I was in here the other night when Tess gave you your bag, and all you said was, "Oh okay, set it over by my keys.""

Billy gave her a defensive stare. *Surely he had thanked Tess for fixing his bag... hadn't he?* He was thankful she had done it. He honestly couldn't remember if he had said the words to her or not.

"She sat here and worked for two hours on it," Abigail said. "And Marvin, too," she added.

"What about Marvin?"

"He goes to that boxing gym every single day of the week and works with you. I wonder if you ever say 'thank you' to him."

"Of course I do," Billy said.

He had told Marvin thank you lots of times. *Hadn't he?* He didn't know for sure now. He tried to think of a time. Surely, he had said it.

"I'm just saying," Abigail said. "My mom and dad didn't let us stand up from the dinner table without thanking them for our food. I just got used to that. Maybe they were overboard, but I think if you're going to mess up one way or the other, it's better to mess up by saying it more. People like to be thanked for things they do."

Billy shrugged casually, but Abigail's words had made him think. He wasn't an ungrateful person, but the truth was, he didn't say those words very often. He considered what she said about their parents teaching them to give thanks, and he realized no one had ever done that for him. He wasn't a 'thank you' type of guy. Until this moment, he didn't think that was a problem.

"Twenty bucks is pretty good for babysitting," he said, still glancing out of the window as he waited for Tess.

"It's amazing," Abigail said. "Back home, I used to get seven bucks for babysitting the Broussards *all* weekend. And little Teddy's a nightmare. He pulled some of my hair out one time."

Billy laughed at the thought. He acted nonchalant and unaffected, but all he could think was how many people he must have offended by not thanking them. He thought about Tess stitching his bag for two hours straight. He didn't even think about how much work she had put into it.

He felt something he had been feeling a lot lately. Conviction. In the past, that word would have scared him, made him put on loud music and start drinking. But not now. He had been convicted of a lot of his behaviors lately, and being with Tess made him choose to confront those things rather than run from them. She believed in him. She believed he could change and be better.

Her confidence in him gave him something to strive for. Having Tess anticipate and expect the best from him caused him to want to tackle his shortcomings rather than run from them.

He decided not to be offended by Abigail's words. He decided he would take them as a challenge and try verbalizing thankfulness for a while—see how it went.

Tess came out of her room a few minutes later wearing shorts and a blouse that was sleeveless and looked more like a bathing suit top than a regular shirt. She was proper, but she was showing just enough skin to drive Billy wild. He wanted to claim her constantly. He wanted to keep a hand on her, let everyone know she was his. And this was even before they left the apartment.

Abigail stayed home while they headed to the beach. They were on their way down the stairs, Billy going down in front of Tess, when Billy stopped in his tracks and turned to face her. Her momentum was already moving forward, and she fell gently into his arms. He was expecting her to do that, so he caught her.

"You okay?" she said.

He smiled at her surprised expression. She was on the step above him, which made her as tall as he was. She stared into his eyes, innocently wondering if everything was all right.

"Did you forget something?" she asked.

"Yeah, I wanted to… I needed to thank you for fixing my bag the other day. I don't know if I ever told you 'thank you' for that."

Her expression softened as she stared at him. "You didn't have to," she said. "I knew you were thankful."

"Well, I should have told you. I shouldn't have made you assume it."

She smiled and leaned toward him, reaching up and touching the side of his face. She stared at Billy like he was the most desirable thing in the world. He had no idea what he had done to deserve Tess Cohen's attention.

"You're welcome," she said.

She leaned in to kiss him on the cheek, which caused his heart to pound violently. There was nothing so sweet as the touch of a woman—the touch of Tess.

"I was happy to sew it for you. It makes me think you'll glance at it sometime when you're training hard and feeling tired, and it'll make you know I'm cheering for you. *Go Billy! You can do it!*" She pumped her fists, acting like she was cheering, but she was whispering and showing silent excitement because they were in a public stairwell.

Billy did not feel like he deserved Tess. He couldn't believe she was able to see past his lack of manners and be so patient with him.

"I'll set my bag where I can see that patch while I'm training," he said.

She nodded. "Good."

"But, thank you for doing it."

"You're welcome, you old sap."

That was it. Tess was teasing him, and Billy didn't take kindly to being teased. She was standing above him, so they were positioned just perfectly so that Billy could easily grab onto her and throw her over his shoulder.

Tess let out a quiet shriek but she held onto him, making it easier for him to handle her weight. He carried her to the bottom of the stairs and set her on her feet in the doorway. She giggled as she stabilized herself.

"I thought you were going to carry me all the way to the beach," she said.

Billy opened the door and gestured to his car, which was parked right in front.

"We're driving to the beach."

***

It was three hours later when Billy showed up at the gym for his workout. He and Tess spent some time at the beach, and now he was ready to get this part of his day over with.

He loved boxing, and he didn't want to quit, but in the moment, he didn't enjoy the hard work. He thought about giving up before and during most workouts, but he never did, and afterward he was always happy with himself for sticking with it.

He took one day at a time. He gave his all at training sessions. He listened to Coach Jones and tried his best, and he could see progress in himself, both mentally and physically. Billy felt stronger as an athlete and as a person. Tess and Marvin were both positive people, and it had rubbed off on Billy. Not that he walked around with a cheesy grin on his face or anything. But he did feel better. Maybe it was just that he had people in his life who believed in him now.

"Hey Easy B," Dizzy said when Billy came into the gym. "Coach wants to see you in his office before you get started today."

"Uh-oh, I'm in trouble," Billy said. But he was smiling. He knew nothing was the matter. It was pretty common for Coach to want to talk to Billy before they got started. Most of the time, he would tell him a specific warmup so that Billy could go ahead and break a sweat. Billy went to Marvin's door and knocked lightly twice with his knuckle.

"Is that Easy?"

"Yes," Billy said.

"Come on in."

Billy walked into Coach's office, standing in the open space, and waiting to hear what his warmup would be.

"Go ahead and have a seat," Marvin said, motioning to the chair that was on the other side of his desk.

Billy listened to his coach, and he stepped in farther and took a seat in the chair. "I'm glad you wanted to talk, actually," Billy said as he sat.

"Oh yeah, why's that?" Marvin asked.

"Because I wanted to talk to you, too."

"All right, well, you can go first," Marvin said.

"Well, now let me make sure yours isn't bad," Billy said. "You're not kicking me out of the gym or anything, are you?"

"What? No. Kicking you out of the gym? No. Why would I do that?"

"Because I was just going to thank you and I thought it might be awkward if you were… but now that I know that you're not… thank you. Thank you so much, Coach."

"Thank me for what?"

"Everything, Coach Marvin. Everything. Thank you for inviting me here and then for teaching me. I know you have other stuff you could be doing half the time when you're working with me, and I just wanted you to know I'm learning a lot."

"Dizzy told you," Marvin said, shaking his head slowly as he looked straight at Billy

"Told me what?"

"Who told you? It had to be Dizzy. Nobody else has seen them."

"Seen what?"

Marvin made a loud scoffing sound. "Don't even come in here being all sentimental and try to tell me you don't know what I got you."

"What'd you get me?" Billy asked.

He was so confused that Marvin tilted his head at Billy.

"You don't know?"

"No," Billy said. "You don't need to get me anything. You shouldn't. I owe you so much already. I'm sorry I haven't come out and said that yet."

"You dying or something?" Marvin asked.

"No," Billy said, laughing a little. "Not that I know of. Someone just told me I should be more thankful, and I think they were right."

"Tess?" Marvin asked.

"Her sister, actually."

"You like that girl, don't you?"

"Yes, wait, who? Tess? Yes." Billy said, staring into space. Him *liking* Tess had to be the biggest understatement that had ever been made. Like wasn't nearly a strong enough word. He loved her. He needed her.

Marvin picked something up. He brought it up over the desk and spread it out across the top. It was a white sweater with black lettering. It had three words on the back, embroidered with fuzzy embroidered block letters.

Easy
Billy
Castro

It looked amazing. It looked so natural that Billy stared at it, wondering if he had seen one just like it before.

But he hadn't.

"Who, what... whose is this?" he asked.

"It's mine," Marvin said. "I'll be wearing this one. I got two more like this. They're for the coaches. Everybody in your corner will have one of these on."

"Oh, I love it. Thank you."

"You'll really thank me when you see this."

Chapter 14

Tess

"And he just handed them to you?" I asked.

"No. First he laid this sweater on the table."

"He got you a sweater?"

"No, I don't have one of those. They're for the coaches. But you should've seen them. They have my name across the back. They're so cool. I almost lost it when I saw that, but then he starts putting other stuff on the table—shoes, gloves, shorts."

"You're kidding. Brand new?"

"Yes, brand new. With my name on it. Custom. He said I'll be ready to take my first amateur match soon and that it might not be very long before I go pro. Can you believe that?"

I let out a nervous breath. "Oh, my goodness, Billy."

I didn't want to see him get into a fight, but at the same time, I knew it was his calling in life, and I knew it was my calling to be next to him. I went over to the couch and sat next to him.

My sister and Evelyn were in the bedroom getting dressed. We had plans to head down to a concert on the boardwalk. It was free, and there was a dance competition, so we had been planning on going.

Billy was tired after training all afternoon, and he had a bruise under his eye from an accidental headbutt with his sparring partner. It was the first thing we talked about when he came in the door. But he assured me he didn't want to cancel our plans.

"Where'd you put them?" I asked. "I want to see."

"Where'd I put what?"

"Your shorts and gloves and all that stuff."

"Oh, they're in my car."

"Abigaillllll, lets goooo!" I yelled out, rushing my sister because I wanted to see his new stuff. This made Billy smile.

Within minutes, we were on our way back to the beach for the concert. Abigail, Evelyn, and I all tried on Billy's new gloves while we were on the way. He loved that I was proud of him and wanted to support him in his dream.

The concert was packed. Radio stations had been promoting the event for days, and there was nothing else going on that weekend. We had to park so far from the boardwalk that we joked about the fact that we should have walked from Bank Street.

We started as a group of four, but by the time we found a place to stand and watch the band, we had turned into a much larger group. Daniel and some of his friends joined us first, then Abigail and Evelyn saw some people they knew, and before long, there were fifteen or twenty of us standing around who were somehow acquainted.

Billy leaned in to speak to me not long after we found a place to settle in and watch the band. "I'm going to get something to drink," he said to me. "Do you want anything?"

"Maybe a soda," I said. "But I'll just share yours. Do you need help?"

"No," Billy said. "I'll be back in a few minutes."

I walked through the group when he left so that I could stand closer to my sister while Billy was away.

"They're good, aren't they?" Abigail said, moving around a little to the beat.

"Do you want to be in the contest, Abby?" Daniel asked, hearing her compliment the band.

"No way!" she said. "I am way too scared for that."

"You're not scared," he said. "You dance all the time."

"*Joking around*," she said in an exaggerated tone. "These people are serious. I saw one lady warming up her hips, doing the Can-can or whatever you call it… that Spanish dance where the hips snap back-and-fourth."

"The Salsa," one of Daniel's friends said.

"The *Salsa*?" Abigail said. "What the heck is that? I thought it's the Cha-cha or something like that."

"No, there's a dance called the Salsa, too," Daniel said, agreeing with his friend.

"All I know is the Twist and the Monkey," Abigail said. "Silly stuff, like the Swim. I can't be in a competition with that."

"I don't see why not," Daniel said. "You could at least just go out there and dance before the contest gets started."

"Maybe later," Abigail said with a shrug.

"I will," Evelyn said.

And she and Daniel made their way onto the boardwalk where everyone was dancing. After Daniel and Evelyn moved, the guy who was standing on the other side of them glanced at us.

"I'm Jacob," he said. "Daniel's cousin."

"Abby," my sister said.

"And I'm Tess."

"I saw you came up with Billy Castro," he said.

"Yeah," I said, nodding and smiling and mostly looking at the band, like the rest of us were doing.

"I would be careful if I were you," Jacob said.

"Of what?" I asked casually, trying not to sound as offended as I was.

"Of Billy. He's... some guys you just don't mess with, and Billy Castro is one of them. I've seen him get in like three fights, and every time, the other guy got knocked out. He's not messing around. I mean, look at him right now. He's got a black eye like he's been fighting."

I was about to stop him. I was about to tell him that he got that black eye by accident while he was training. But he leaned in closer to continue speaking to me before I could say anything.

"And I heard his mom was some psychopath who killed his dad and then herself. People like that are just… it's better to stay away from them. You never know what he'll do."

"You never know what *anybody* will do," I said, snapping back at him.

"What?" he asked, startled.

"You never know what *anybody* will do," I said. "I might be the one to knock somebody out if they hurt someone I love."

"Yeah, but you weren't raised in a house where—"

"How do you know anything about what kind of house Billy was raised in?" I asked, staring straight at the guy.

"I don't. I just know what I heard."

"And what do you stand to gain?"

"What?" he asked, looking confused.

"What do you stand to gain from talking about him when he walks off?" I asked.

"Nothing. That's why you shouldn't be so mad. I'm just trying to help you."

"I'm not mad. I'm just saying, you shouldn't talk about people you don't know. I know Billy's whole story, and I know that what you said earlier is not even true. You're misinformed."

"All right, fine," Jacob said, raising his hands in surrender. "I was only trying to help.

"Thank you, I guess, but Billy's a really good person. He did go through some stuff, but that was a long time ago. And he's about to get famous, so if I were you, I'd try to make friends with him now, anyway."

"What's he getting famous for?"

"He's a fighter," I said. "Boxing."

"Oh, over there on Bank Street with Daniel?"

"Yeah," I said. "That's what the black eye's about."

"Billy's really good," Abigail said, interjecting. "We go over there at the end of his practice sometimes. He's serious about it. They've got t-shirts and shorts with his name on it. He just got brand new gloves."

"Did you see that?" Daniel said, when he and Evelyn eventually left the dance floor to come back and stand near us again. "We didn't know what we were doing and we were just fine out there." He was obviously talking to Abigail.

"Are you not going to leave me alone until I dance with you?"

"No, I'm not," Daniel said.

Abigail took a deep resigned breath. "Fine," she said.

Some of their other friends joined us, and Evelyn started talking to them.

Jacob looked at me with a shrug. "I think we got off on the wrong foot," he said. "I'm Jacob."

"Tess," I said.

145

"Would you want to dance?"

"Oh, thank you, but I promised—"

"She's dancing with me." Billy's voice came from behind me. He stepped in close to me, putting a possessive hand on my side. He took a sip out of his cup before handing it to me. I took a sip. It was iced tea, but I barely tasted it because I was so infatuated with him, and it took my breath away to have him stand beside me and share a drink from the same cup.

Billy reached out and handed that almost empty cup to Jacob who took it even though he was confused. Then Billy pulled me to the dance floor. The band was playing a medium tempo song, and Billy walked into the group of dancers before pulling me close. It wasn't officially a slow dance, but the song was groovy enough that he held me close, like you would in a slow dance.

I held onto him, looking at him, letting him lead me. I had experienced the pleasure of dancing with Billy before. He had natural rhythm and he moved smoothly, swaying, pulling me along with him. I held onto his mid-section trying but failing to ignore the way his muscle-lined torso moved and flexed. I could never be as attracted to another man as I was to Billy.

If you had asked me a year ago, I might have said I didn't believe in soul mates. Abigail, on the other hand, firmly believes that Jim Morrison is going to be in the same elevator as her one day, and they'll fall madly in love. I would have told you there was no such thing. But that was what happened with me and Billy. I knew Billy was the one from the first moment. The feeling of being next to him was magical.

The music was loud, and people were everywhere, bumping up against us, sweating and swaying in the humid, salty evening air.

"You weren't going to dance with that guy, were you?"

"No," I said, holding onto him. "I don't dance with anybody but you."

He held me closer. "What'd he say to you, besides asking you to dance?"

"He said he went to high school with you. He said he saw you get in a few fights and how tough you were."

"He did not say that."

"Well, I'm paraphrasing. He said nobody should mess with you because he's seen you in a few fights and the other guys always got knocked out. He thought your bruise was from a street fight."

"What'd you say?" Billy asked.

"I said you were training at Marvin's. That you were going to be a famous boxer. I told him he should ask for your autograph."

Billy smiled and shook his head. "No, you didn't."

"Not the autograph part, but I did say you were about to get famous."

Billy laughed and then made a confused smirk. "And he still asked you to dance?"

"I know," I said. "I don't know what he was thinking."

He held me close, moving to the slow but steady rhythm. It was a hot summer evening, and the boardwalk was packed with dancers. Billy just held me there, moving with me in his arms. The music was bass-y and fluid, and Billy knew how to move. I was breathless, caught-up, spinning, swimming, swaying in a dreamy sort of bliss.

Billy kissed me. He did it right there on the boardwalk, not caring who was around. We moved slowly and then he leaned down and touched his mouth to mine. He held me tight, and he kissed me good. It was hot outside, and my blood was thick and warm. Billy knew how to drive me crazy. He knew how to dance, and he especially knew how to kiss. He wasn't causing a scene, but it was a tender and intimate connection for such a chaotic atmosphere. I didn't care. I loved that Billy wanted to kiss me in a crowd. He gave me a sweltering, gut-flipping gentle open-mouthed kiss that made me weak in the knees.

Billy grinned at me as he pulled back. The song ended, and the band went right into another one with a similar tempo, keeping us moving. He was masculine and hard as a rock, and I felt all stirred-up inside as a result of touching his body while it was in motion. Goodness.

"I don't think I'm going back to Louisiana, come August," I said.

Chapter 15

One month later

Abigail would, no doubt, find her way to Albert's room as soon as we walked into Billy's house. She loved Jimmy, Albert's squirrel, and she knew how to get him out of his cage and put him back even if Albert wasn't home. Albert's car was in the driveway, but you never knew with that guy.

One of Matty's brothers was sitting on the porch at the house next door, and he saw us outside as we were walking up. He yelled over at Billy.

Abigail kept walking and went into Billy's. I tried to leave with her. I pulled away from Billy, trying to break contact so that he could stay out there and talk to Anthony alone, but Billy kept a hold of my hand. I was happy that he always wanted me with him, and I didn't protest any further. I stayed by his side and walked with him over to Matty's to talk to Anthony.

It was late July. It was hot, and the sun was high in the sky. I held a hand over my eyes to shield them from the bright light as I looked upward at Anthony, who hadn't moved from his chair on the porch.

"Did Matty talk to you?" Anthony said.

"Uh, I talked to him yesterday," Billy said in an uncertain tone.

"Cause we were talking about you not running errands for him anymore."

"Yeah, I went down to part-time so I can train. I'm just doing some construction for him now."

It didn't surprise me to hear Billy say any of this. A couple of weeks ago, Billy had talked to Matty about scaling back on his responsibilities. Billy wanted to continue working for Matty's construction crew, but he was done with the errands.

"Yeah, well, me and Matty were talking about that, and seeing as how Tony's been picking up your slack, Matty was saying he was gonna let Tony move into the house."

"What house?" Billy said.

"Your house."

"We don't have a room."

"You have *your* room," Anthony said chuckling.

Tony was Anthony's son, so it made sense that he was looking after him, but he came across as a jerk.

"Matty said that room was part of your deal," Anthony added, shrugging.

"It was part of my deal, but I'm paying more rent on it now. That's why I'm doing the construction. I worked that out with Matty a couple of weeks ago."

"Well, I guess he hasn't talked to you yet, but things have changed. You know, with Tony taking over how he is, Matty wants him close by."

"So, he's giving Tony my room?" Billy asked.

"Yeah," Anthony said. He pulled a cigarette out of a box and lit it.

"When did he tell you this?" Billy asked.

"I just talked to him this morning."

Billy looked past him, into the house. "Is he home?"

"No. I don't know where he is. I was supposed to meet him to see if your old bed was good enough, or if we needed to get Tony something else. Is the mattress in there yours, or are you leaving it here?"

"Are you here right now to come in my house and look at my bed?" Billy asked in a calm tone.

"I'm gonna wait for Matty and we'll go in together."

"Okay," Billy said. He spoke hesitantly like he was at a loss for words.

"I guess you're trying to get serious with this boxing stuff," Anthony said just as Billy was turning to walk away.

"Yeah," Billy agreed, nodding.

"I heard you have a fight up in Houston."

"How'd you hear about that?" Billy said. "I just found out about it yesterday."

"Matty knows everything," Anthony said. He let out a wheezy laugh. "He said we might have to bet against you, just this once. He said he could see you doing okay as a boxer one of these days, but he knows something about that guy they're putting you up against from Houston. I think he's eight and one as an amateur. He's just got way more experience.

He should have already gone pro by now. Matty said Marvin should have never put you up against... never mind," Anthony said, shaking his head. "I know he thinks you'll do all right eventually."

"Thanks," Billy said as he turned to walk away. He said it sincerely enough, but I could tell that he was guarded. *How could he not be?* Anthony Stills was perhaps the rudest person I had ever met. I could not believe he had said some of those things to Billy just now. Matty had been the only father figure in Billy's life for years, and here comes Anthony, announcing casually that Matty was kicking him out of his house *and* betting against him in his first fight.

The part about betting against Billy was unbelievable to me. That just didn't need to be said. I was fuming as a result of the interaction with Anthony, but I pretended to be calm for Billy's sake.

I smiled at him as we walked into the door. I knew he needed me in this moment, and I wanted to say and do exactly the right thing to let him know I was proud of him and that he was on the right track.

I glanced at him as we walked to his room. "Marvin wouldn't put you in a situation if he didn't think you were ready for it," I said.

Billy let out a casual chuckle. "I know," he said. "I'm not worried about Anthony. He's always trying to push my buttons."

Billy was being a little too casual for the degree of unnerving news Anthony had just given him.

"What are you going to do about a room?"

153

"I don't know. I don't know when they'll try to have Tony move in. It's really the first I've heard of any of this."

"I live across the street from the gym," I said.

I had not planned on saying that. I just opened my mouth, and the words came out.

"What's that mean?" Billy asked.

"Daniel's leaving next week," I continued. "The Kings will be looking for some help around the store. You could maybe work there with me part-time and be right across the street so you can train any time you want." I shrugged nervously, realizing the gravity of what I was proposing. "I, just, with Matty and everything, I didn't know if you even wanted to work construction with him anymore, and if not, you know, I just wanted to try to think of... I was thinking about Daniel leaving, and the store being right there across the street from the gym."

Billy stared at me patiently until I stopped rambling and then he gave me a slow grin. Light from the window was streaming into the room, and Billy was smiling down at me like I was the object of his desire. His expression was thoughtful, sweet and so handsome. The whole scene was gorgeous.

"Are you saying you want me to work with you and live with you?" Billy asked, as if making sure he understood correctly.

"Yeah, that's what I'm saying. Hopefully, between both of us, we can make rent and bills and then work on our own stuff, too. I can paint while you're at the gym."

Billy didn't respond right away, so I kept talking nervously.

"I know it's a lot to think about, and it probably seems soon, and I'll be totally fine if you decided you don't think it's a good idea for us to—"

I stopped talking when Billy reached up and gently covered my mouth with his hand. He just did it long enough to get me to be quiet. We smiled at each other during a few seconds of silence.

"Yes," he said nodding calmly, slowly.

He took me by the arm and pulled me gently to him, the front of our bodies touching just a little.

"Yes to what?" I asked, staring up at his jaw.

"Yes to all of that," he said.

"Well, I wasn't quite done," I said. "Unfortunately, there's a catch."

"What's the catch?"

"My parents will expect us to get married first. They're not really the type who could live with me not getting married before I—"

"Why's that unfortunate?" Billy asked.

"Because I didn't think you'd want to get married so soon," I said. I felt vulnerable as a result of our candid conversation, but now that we were this far in, I had to push myself to speak my mind.

"Tess, I want to marry you. I desperately do. I would have married you on that first day if I would have known things would have ended up like this."

Billy paused and took my hands, positioning them around his mid-section, telling me just how and where to hold onto him. He was flirting with me, making me touch him.

"You should really be going home next month to marry Spencer Henderson, but instead, you'll stay here and marry me, and I'm not going to do a thing to stop you."

"Who is Spencer Henderson?" I said, glancing at him with a look of confusion.

"Abigail told me all about that guy your mom wants you to marry back home."

I let out a little laugh. "Stephen," I said.

Billy scowled at me playfully when I said that name, and I smiled.

"Too bad for him, anyway, though," he said with a shrug. "It's too late. You've already got yourself engaged over in Galveston."

I scanned his face, staring up at him breathlessly. "I have, haven't I?"

"And to a fighter, no less."

I put my hand lightly on his chest. "A warrior," I said, staring at him. "A champion."

"*Knock, knock!*" Matty called. We heard his gravelly voice as he came in, and Billy and I braced ourselves but didn't let each other go.

"What's happening, Easy-Billy?" Matty said the nickname slowly and with some deeper meaning. I didn't know what he was trying to say. I thought maybe he didn't like the name, or maybe he was jealous that Billy was going by a name Marvin gave him. Either way, he said it funny.

"Yep," Billy said casually.

"Anthony said he told you about Big Tony moving in here."

"Yeah," Billy agreed. "He said you were coming here to look at the bed or something."

"Hey, Billy, I'm not kicking you out on the street," Matty said. "I want you to stay on the couch as long as you need. You can even come over to my house and stay on my couch. I just needed to open up this bedroom for big T since he's working for me now. I can't have him living all the way in Bayou Vista when I need him for something."

"I understand," Billy said confidently.

"But, like I said, you can just move your stuff into the living room or in there with one of those other guys. I'm giving Tony this room because, you know, the window's right here on this side where he can look out for my place."

"It's okay. I understand. I have somewhere to go," Billy said. "When's Tony planning on moving in?"

"Where do you have to go?" Matty asked.

"When do I need to be out?" Billy said without answering the other question.

"I told him on the first."

"That's next week," Billy said.

"Yeah, but I'm not kicking you out, Billy."

157

"I'm going to look at the bed," Anthony said, cutting in. Matty gave him a nod, but none of us cared.

"I know you're not kicking me out," Billy said, with the confidence of a man who knew he had somewhere to go. "It works out, actually."

"Why's that? What do you mean it works out?" Matty asked the question while he was looking back and forth between Billy and me.

"Because I was talking about moving in with Tess."

I smiled and nodded a little backing Billy up when Matty glanced at me.

"We were talking about getting married," Billy said.

"*Mar-ried*," Matty returned dramatically. His face was a mask of confusion. "I thought you just met a couple months ago."

"We did," Billy said. "But sometimes, Matty, there's just not a way to avoid marrying a girl. And this happens to be one of those times. She's willing to marry me, and I'd regret it for the rest of my life if I didn't do it."

Matty just stared at Billy, not knowing what to say.

"Nice place," Anthony yelled, from the top of the stairs, completely oblivious to our conversation.

"Billy here's, getting married," Matty yelled back.

"Oh, congrats," Anthony said, nodding and speaking loudly. "Is this the lucky lady?"

"Yes," Billy said.

Chapter 16

Billy

Three weeks later

Billy and Tess decided to wait a short time to get married. Billy talked to Marvin about everything, and they came up with a plan. Instead of eloping with her instantly so that he could move into the apartment, Billy held off for a few weeks.

He decided it might be wiser to wait for several reasons. It wouldn't come as such a huge shock if they at least let her family know a little ahead of time. Plus, Billy could focus on training for his first match. It was an amateur bout scheduled for the third weekend in August, and he and Tess would get married two days after it occurred.

He would compete on Friday night in Houston. Then he and Tess would travel to her small town of Starks, Louisiana where they would get married the following Sunday in a ceremony with her family and friends.

That would give Billy all of one day to recover from his fight, but he didn't anticipate that it would take that long. He was so confident about it that he promised Tess he wouldn't even get a black eye. But

Tess didn't give him any pressure. She seemed to love that he had a warrior's spirit, and she was looking forward to the grab bag groom she'd be getting as a result of the timing of his fight.

They would say their vows in the small Baptist church where Tess had been dedicated and baptized as a child. Then they would travel back to Galveston where they would set up their life as a couple in that apartment down on Bank Street.

Billy had stayed at Marvin's for the past three weeks while he was training. Marvin lived upstairs from the gym, and he had a nice apartment with an extra bedroom. He insisted that Billy stay with him, and Billy and Tess both agreed that it'd be a good idea so that everything wasn't quite so rushed.

But three weeks passed, and that fated Friday night rolled around faster than either of them thought it would.

Billy found himself in the blue corner locker room.

Just beyond these walls, there was a packed auditorium. Billy was confident and focused, and somehow, at the same time, full of panic and self-doubt. He experienced waves of emotion where he would suddenly feel like he might walk into the ring and lose it in front of the crowd and pass out. Or maybe his body would just refuse to perform. A wave of fear and self-doubt would be followed with one of confidence and self-assurance.

Billy remained silent and stoic through it all. He trusted his training. He trusted that Marvin knew what he could handle. He did his best to remain calm and loose. He thought of Tess and what she had said to him before he left for Houston. She assured him she didn't care what happened in this match. She made a whole speech about being in love with him and her feelings not being affected by his ability to box or the outcome of this match.

She would be in the audience, watching him. Tess, Abigail, and several other people from the gym made the trip up to Houston to watch. Billy had fought lots of times, but never like this. He went through some sparring situations during training where Marvin invited everyone in the gym, and even a few off the street to watch so that Billy would get a little taste of what it was like to perform in front of spectators. But he didn't know how he would react once he actually got out there in front of a real crowd.

It was almost time.

Someone came into the locker room and announced that the fight before his had just ended and it would only be a minute until they were ready. Marvin came to stand in front of Billy. He looked Billy in the eyes and spoke calmly to him.

"Somewhere in the Bible, Billy, in one of the gospels, Luke, I think, Jesus was in this big, huge crowd of people. His mom and brothers came to see Him, and they were having trouble approaching Him because it was so crowded. And people told Him, *hey, your mom and brothers are here to see you.* And do you know what Jesus said?"

"What?"

"He said that His mother and brothers were those who hear God's word and do it."

Billy blinked, having no idea what any of this meant.

"Do you know what that tells me, Billy?"

"What?"

"That I am His favorite. You see what I'm saying? He feels the same about *me* as He does about His own family—the people He walked with on this earth and loved dearly. It tells me *I'm* His favorite. And, as His favorite, He gives me power and might—strength I shouldn't have. He helps me do things I shouldn't be capable of."

Billy made a noise in his throat as he contemplated.

"And do you know what else it means?" Marvin asked.

"What?"

"That you are His favorite, too. That's one of those amazing, mind-boggling things that God can do and we can't. We can only have one favorite of something. That's the whole meaning of the word. But God, He can bend the rules. He can bend language and science and do all sorts of things we can't. He actually loves me as much as He loved that family He grew up with, and He loves you as much as He loves me. That's a fact, Jack. It's written right there in plain English, words of Christ in red ink." Marvin slapped Billy's shoulders, a hearty whack before shaking him getting him pumped. "This means exciting things, Easy Billy. It means that you can go out there knowing that God Almighty is with you, that He loves you, that you're his favorite. You hear me?"

"Yes, sir," Billy said with a nod.

Marvin grabbed Billy's head and hugged him. "You're unstoppable. You're relentless, Billy. Powerful. You were destined for greatness. You were born for this. One day, the people out there will be bragging about how they saw you in your first fight. Be gracious, be humble, just breathe and have fun out there, okay?"

Billy nodded.

"I'm proud of you, Easy. Let's take it home, all right?"

"Blue corner, we're ready for you!" a man yelled, opening the door. He peered into the room and gave Billy and Marvin a nod when he saw them headed his way.

One foot in front of the other, Billy marched through the door, down the hallway, into the auditorium, past the crowd and into the ring. Billy thought he would block out the crowd, but he didn't. He took them in during his swimmy, hazy, dreamlike entrance to the ring.

Matty was the first familiar face he took in. Matty's crew was in a big group in the back. Tess. Billy felt a bump in his adrenaline when he saw her. She was smiling. There were others, too, quite a few people he recognized. He said a prayer just before he was announced.

"Easy Billy Cas-trooo!" rolled off of the announcer's tongue like it was a name that had been used since the dawn of time. Billy felt easy. He felt happy and at peace.

The round began. Time seemed to slow down for Billy. He felt like he spent three seconds in everyone else's one second. From the moment the bell rang, he was in a different time space. He heard his own thoughts, and the static sound of his own blood rushing.

This guy was slow.

He threw some punches, but Billy evaded them all. He was only going at about sixty percent where this guy was going for the knock out. Billy's opponent was fully convinced that the fight would end in the first few minutes. He wasn't prepared to go the distance. He was not saving enough energy for that.

Billy thought the most humane thing to do would be to put him out of his misery early rather than messing with him and prolonging things.

The guy landed a punch or two, but they were brushes because Billy saw them coming from a mile away and was able to easily get out of the way. This guy had a good amateur record, but he was no match for Billy. He left himself open. He was slow and predictable.

Billy landed a straight left jab in an effort to get the guy to start blocking his face. It took two of those annoying jabs, but he finally put his hands up. The instant his arm went up to block, Billy shifted his weight forward. He locked his left arm into a curved position and pivoted, delivering a devastating left hook to his opponent's right side.

Marvin had gone into great detail discussing human anatomy, and Billy knew just how and where to place his fist. It took a second or two for the pain to register, but suddenly, Billy's opponent's face changed, and he folded, crumpled, and fell like a wet towel.

Everyone could see the surprise and confusion when the guy first felt the physical effects of the liver shot. There was no shame in collapsing. Billy had been hit in the liver himself—more than once. He knew that blow could end a fight, and tonight it had.

The referee counted to ten, and the opponent stayed on the mat, unable to get up, unable to continue.

The next moments seemed to pass in a blurry, emotion-filled haze. Marvin and Dizzy came into the ring to congratulate Billy. He glanced out at the crowd. There were mixed reactions. Some people looked confused, some happy, some indifferent.

Billy was only searching for a familiar face. He was searching for Tess.

Marvin and Dizzy came up next to him, congratulating him, patting him on the back. But they were quickly announced as the winning side and ushered away since there was a long night of boxing and Billy was not even close to the main event. Once that was done, they walked through the crowd and backstage.

"You did real good, Billy, but we can't stay and talk about it right now. We've got James and Quentin coming up," Dizzy said. "So, me and Coach need to get over to them."

Billy wasn't surprised to hear Dizzy say that. Two of his other gym mates were on the card that night. Billy's had been the first match of the three. He knew the coaches had other guys to worry about.

"What about Tess?" Billy asked.

"She might come back here and wait for you," Dizzy said, pointing at the curtain they were about to go behind. A guy reached out and held it back so Billy and the coaches could walk through. "And if she doesn't, you can go find her in her seat." Dizzy smiled as he scanned Billy's appearance. "It's not like you have injuries to take care of."

Coach Marvin turned and reached up, taking Billy by the head as soon as they made it behind the curtain. He hugged him, patting the back of his head.

"I'm proud of you, Billy," he said.

"Thanks, Coach. Thanks for everything. I'm ready to get back in the ring as soon as possible. Whatever comes up next—just sign me up."

Marvin laughed and patted Billy on the shoulder. "Next time I see you, you'll be a married man."

"Yes, sir."

"All right. Well, I gotta get over to Quentin, but I love you, boy. I truly do. And I'm proud of you. You looked beautiful out there." He patted him again. "If you don't stay till after, I'll see you next week."

Billy nodded. "I'll see you next week, Coach. Thank you."

Chapter 17

Tess

I had no idea what happened in the fight. One minute, Billy was stepping back and defending while the other guy went full-speed, and the next thing I knew, the other guy was balled-up and lying on the mat.

I was looking through my fingers, thinking Billy was in trouble with the way his opponent was going crazy, so I missed what happened. There was a scramble and a series of punches, and all of a sudden, the referee was counting.

I was sitting with my sister and quite a few others who knew Billy. The longer the referee counted, the more our section celebrated. By the time the ref counted to ten, we were all cheering and slapping each other.

The boys were exclaiming something about a *liver shot* as they celebrated, so I figured that had something to do with ending the match.

"I'm going to meet Billy in the back," I said.

"Are we leaving right now?" Abigail asked.

"No. I don't think so. Wait here. I'll come back for you if Billy decides he wants to get on the road."

I waited at a curtain for Billy to appear. I tried to go behind it, but the guy told me it was only for athletes and coaches. He assured me this was the only exit from the locker rooms, and I waited patiently, nervously. I was happy and relieved, but my stomach was still tied in knots from all the adrenaline and excitement. I was able to see the ring from where I was standing. The next match was just getting started, and I watched the action as I waited for Billy.

I had no idea if it was ten seconds or ten minutes that I stood there waiting for Billy.

Then he finally appeared.

He came out alone, and he was dressed in jeans and a t-shirt. His hair was combed back. He looked fresh and clean, and best of all, happy. He talked to the guy who was watching the curtain. Billy smiled, and it looked like he thanked the guy for a compliment, but I had moved to the side and was standing too far over to hear them.

I didn't want Billy to miss seeing me and walk by, so I started heading his way. He caught sight of me when he turned away from the guy at the curtain, and I felt happy and relieved when I saw him smile at me.

Billy had a bag slung over his shoulder, but it didn't stop him from walking straight up to me and taking me into his arms. He picked me up and walked with me in his arms so that we were a little further off to the side. He set me down, and I stared up at him. He was larger than life. I was starstruck. I couldn't stop myself from reaching up to touch a strand of his hair.

"There were a few fights before yours, and just so you know, you were the best one. Looks and skill and everything. You're in a league of your own, Billy. You looked so good with your movements, your smoothness, and you were also the most handsome in your shorts, by far."

Billy laughed.

"I'm so proud of you," I said. "Seriously, you looked like a pro out there."

"Thank you," he said. He grabbed me, giving me a tight hug followed by a kiss on the cheek. "Let's go watch a few more fights and then drive to Louisiana."

Billy knew where we had been sitting, so he led me that way. He held my hand and we walked to the place where our crew from Galveston had a cheering section. Everyone was excited to see Billy, and they all stopped watching the current match while they patted him on the back and congratulated him. He handled himself with a mixture of humbleness and confidence that was perfect and oh so very attractive.

He pulled me close while we sat, watching the next matches. Billy was consumed with becoming a success, and this meant that he stared at every match, dissecting the fighters' movements, taking in their choices, their reactions, analyzing everything. I was proud of him. I liked watching Billy watch boxing more than I liked watching boxing.

He wanted to stay for the whole event, and I didn't mind at all. I placed a collect call to my parents, telling them to leave the door unlocked since we'd be arriving in the middle of the night.

***

Billy slept in my bedroom and I slept in my sister's room with her. I woke up at 9am, and it took several minutes for me to get my bearings and figure out what day it was, where I was, and what I was doing.

I left Abigail sleeping in her bed without disturbing her. I stopped in the bathroom to splash some water on my face and brush my teeth, but I didn't change out of my pajamas, which were a set of shorts and a cap sleeve button down top. I had on those and my house slippers when I left the bathroom.

My parents' house wasn't huge. I could hear them talking in the kitchen. I stood in the hallway, hesitating, wondering what I should do next. I almost headed out to the kitchen where my parents were, but instead I decided to go to my bedroom.

I cautiously, lightly tapped on the door before cracking it open. Billy was sleeping on his side. There was enough light in the room that I could see him lying in my bed. I crept in quietly, closing the door behind me. I tiptoed over to him, smiling at

172

him. His eyes were cracked open and he was smiling sleepily back at me.

"Good morning," he said, moaning.

"Good morning," I whispered.

He was under the covers, his black hair a stark contrast to my white sheets and pillowcase. I could not help myself. I had to lie next to him. Quickly, so I wouldn't lose the nerve, I hopped onto the bed. I stretched out next to Billy, and he turned and flung the covers off of himself and over me, wrapping me up like I was in a cocoon. He flung his leg and arm over me, holding me tightly, trapping me in his blanket-lined embrace.

"What happened?" I said, laughing. "How did I get like this?"

I squirmed with delight, and Billy flexed his legs and arms, holding me tighter. I made a quiet noise of approval in my chest—one that sounded like a whimper mixed with a sigh—and I snuggled into him.

"Tomorrow I get to wake up with you in my bed," Billy said, moaning sleepily, holding me close.

"Not tomorrow, but the next day," I said.

Billy shifted in discontentment when I said that, and I smiled.

"I'm marrying you tomorrow," I said. "But I won't wake up in your bed till the next morning, remember? I'll sleep in Abigail's room again tonight."

Billy made a moaning sound of disapproval that made me smile.

"What day is it?" he asked.

"Saturday," I said.

"Let's just get married today," he said.

"We can't. We have people who are expecting to come to it tomorrow."

"Can't we just call them and get them to move it up a day?" he asked.

"No, no, you can't," I said in a serious but silly tone. "My mom hasn't even finished my dress."

"What do you mean? She better hop to it."

"She's almost done," I said. "It's just a few final touches."

"You don't need a special dress to get married, anyway. I'll marry you in this little number you have on right now. This looks good to me."

I reached out of the covers and gently put my hand on the side of his face. "You didn't get a black eye for our wedding."

"Are you disappointed?" he asked.

"No. Never. I don't want to see you get hurt. I'd much rather you not get touched in a fight, like last night."

"That won't happen the further up I go in the chain."

"I know," I said. "But maybe if you could just come out and hit them with that side punch every time like you did last night. I loved that one. That made it go quick and easy for everybody."

Billy laughed, still holding me. "It wasn't easy for him, believe me."

"I know, but it could have been a lot worse," I said. "Even for him, right?"

"Yeah, you're right," he said, smiling like he was amused by me.

I came really close to saying that Matty must be sad that he bet on the other guy, but I decided not to bring that up. I already had my mouth open to speak, so I had to come up with something else to say.

"My mom had a great idea," I said.

"What?"

"They came to the apartment yesterday to get the rest of Abigail's things, and they ended up taking all of my paintings back with them."

"Here? Why?" Billy asked.

I had completed eight paintings since I had moved to Galveston. I had several more works in progress, but eight of them were complete. I was hanging onto them until I felt like it was a cohesive collection and then I would start to try to sell them. Billy knew all of this, so he was curious when I said my parents took them to Louisiana.

"Just for the wedding," I said. "My mom said we should hang them in the reception hall. They can easily take down the paintings that are already there and hang mine in their place. Mom said people would like seeing them since they're so representative of my life in Galveston."

"They'll probably want to buy them," Billy said.

"Maybe," I agreed, feeling excited at the thought. I had done some paintings while living in Louisiana, but none were as good as my beach scene paintings. I loved my surroundings there, and it showed in my art. I had improved a lot simply because I was in love with the landscape and architecture, and I wanted to try my hardest to do them justice.

"Tess, do you know that last night was just the first of many nights I'm going to spend competing?" he asked.

I nodded. He was looking straight at me when he asked, so I didn't have to answer out loud.

"There's going to be a lot of nights at the gym, and a lot in the ring."

"I know," I said. "I already know what I'm doing, Billy, who I'm marrying. I didn't think that just because you're getting married you have to quit boxing and put on a suit and tie and become an accountant."

"Yeah, I can pretty much promise I'll never turn into an accountant."

I laughed, and he pushed his chin forward and kissed me while I was still smiling. He pulled back slowly. Our lips got stuck together. I had this wonderful wave of yearning like I wanted to unbutton him and crawl inside. I couldn't wait until he was my husband.

"Two days away," I said.

"More like one-and-a-half," Billy returned.

"Are you scared?" I asked.

"Are you?" he asked.

"I asked you first."

"No," he said. "Are you?"

"No," I said. I stared at him. "Is that bad?"

"No. Why would it be?" he asked.

"I don't know. Aren't you supposed to be nervous and terrified when you're about to make the biggest, most important commitment of your life?"

"Not when it's the right one," he said, easily. He hesitated, looking at me with an expression that changed to one of nonchalance as he shrugged. "But if you don't want to do it..." he trailed off and moved, beginning to shift his body like he was going to look away from me. He was messing with me, but I scrambled to reach out and hold him. I grasped him through the blanket.

"Wait, wait, wait, I do... I'm not nervous. I'm not scared. I was just saying it's weird that we're not."

Billy smiled and held onto me again since he had been joking all along. "I don't think it's weird," he said. "I think that's how it should be. I think we make our own rules. We're the ones sitting here, having the feelings," he shrugged. "We may as well make them good ones."

Chapter 18

My mom made my wedding dress. It was a long, straight, simple white dress with lace, and she did a gorgeous job. I wore nude panty hose and two-inch heels. I styled my hair in a smooth but full hairstyle that hung over my shoulders. I had only hair-sprayed my hair a few other times in front of Billy, but those times, Abigail had helped me. My sister was good at styling hair, but this time, I had Caroline Ackerman, my mom's hairstylist for thirty years, available to help.

I was worried that she'd have me looking too stiff, but she didn't at all. She gave me Jean Shrimpton hair with side-swept bangs, and she helped me put on the veil just the right way. That was earlier, and now all I had to do was get to the church and put on my dress.

My mom cried three different times while I was getting my hair done, and I had to make her leave the room. I had always cried easy, and seeing other people cry was a sure way to get me to smear my mascara.

I thought about having Abigail and a good friend of mine from school stand up with me and be my bridesmaids, but I decided not to do it. Billy hadn't invited anyone to the wedding, and I didn't care about all that, anyway. It was official enough based on the fact that I was wearing white and we were saying vows.

***

And now it was time.

Our church was small, but there was an organ, and the regular church organist was there to play. I heard the beginning of the wedding march, and my Uncle Al smiled at me and opened the door that led to the sanctuary. I was standing next to my father, holding onto his arm. I glanced at him, and could see through my veil that he was staring back at me, looking proud. I smiled, but glanced away quickly for fear that I would start crying already.

At least I had the veil to shield me a little. It wasn't much, but there were three layers of tulle between me and the rest of the world, and I was thankful for it.

Hot, stinging tears sprang to my eyes the instant I turned the corner and saw all the people in the church. I was expecting a small crowd, but there must have been a hundred people. The right side was filled with people from Galveston. Matty and two rows of guys from his crew, along with Marvin, Dizzy, and several others from the gym. Daniel had already left for the Army, but his parents and sister had even come.

I was shocked to find the Kings, Matty Sims, and Marvin Jones all sitting in my church. I could not believe all of these people had made the long trip to Louisiana to be here. This was truly a surprise to me. It was impossible to stop myself from crying. I held my bouquet in the hand that was looped around my father's arm so that I could use my free hand to catch my tears with a tissue that was strategically folded and kept in my hand for this very moment.

It was just too much seeing the church full of our family and friends and seeing the way they stood up and looked at me as I walked past. I tried to keep my face neutral, but tears fell. My dad saw me crying and he leaned into me, giving me support and distraction. I glanced at him and smiled through the tears.

I had not made eye contact with Billy yet. I dreaded it because I thought I might lose it and start to bawl. I was already on the verge of losing it as it was. I had to do it. I had to look at my man. I was a quarter of the way down the aisle, and I had to look at him.

I knew where he was standing, and my eyes found him and locked on his eyes. Billy was smiling at me, but I could tell he didn't quite see that my eyes had just found his. I realized it was probably hard to see the details of my face from a distance. The closer I got, the more his smile grew.

Billy was wearing a dark grey suit with a white shirt and a small bowtie. He was dashing, and he was looking straight at me. I cried and wiped the corners of my eyes with the tissue. Billy's smile broadened when he saw me dabbing again.

My dad let me go and gave Billy a hug once we arrived at the front.

Those moments were surreal, dreamlike.

The pastor said some words, and I mostly did my best to answer correctly and not pass out. There wasn't much *enjoying the moment* for me. I enjoyed it, don't get me wrong. It wasn't *unenjoyable* by any means. But I wasn't able to relax and take in the ceremony. I was nervous and full of emotion, and because of that, the ceremony passed in a happy but blurry haze.

I knew I was doing the right thing, though.

Billy was unbelievably dashing, and I was in love with him for the man he was on the inside as well as the outside. He had grown and changed so much since I had known him. I couldn't wait to spend the rest of my life getting to know him and seeing what he was capable of.

We said vows, and Billy lifted my veil before kissing me. Matty had a ruckus crew, and they whooped and hollered, which caused my Aunt Mildred to gasp. It was wonderful. I loved our wedding so much. It was simple and short, and perhaps the most perfect wedding there had ever been.

Billy and I were inseparable during the reception. He held me close, not taking his hand off of me even when he was talking to other people.

There were snacks, and we all stood around enjoying some food while mingling and having conversation. The Galveston people more or less stayed with Galveston people and the same with the folks from Starks.

Marvin was the character who brought both sides together. Everyone knew about Marvin Jones, and my friends and family were all excited that he would come to our little town.

It was an unlikely group of people, and we made sure to take a big group photo after we cut the cake and before people started leaving.

Matty and his group were the first to leave.

He told Billy on his way out that Anthony only said he was betting against him to make Billy fight harder. He said that he was betting on Billy from the beginning and knew he wasn't going to lose that match. Billy told Matty he knew Anthony was lying, and they got into a good-natured shoving match because of it.

The Kings were the next to leave, and some of my friends and family left at that time.

Billy got everyone's attention after they headed out and before anyone else could leave.

"I'm not much of a person who, you know, makes speeches..." He trailed off, making a face like he was thinking about something. "But I also don't usually find myself in a situation where I'm getting married."

This caused everyone to laugh, and Billy smiled and looked at me sweetly before glancing out at our friends and family again.

"Sometimes, life just seems to go on day after day without much change at all. It's like things just feel like they'll always be the same. And then, other times, everything happens so quickly that it's hard to keep up—to even tell which *way* is up. (People laughed.) But really, it's hard to believe the shifts and changes that came at me so fast. That's where I've been lately. In the last few months, my entire life has made this huge turn, and I find myself on a completely different path than the one I was on. I have people in my life who are investing in me and giving me their trust." Billy gave a nod to Marvin before turning to face me again. "And you," he said. "You, Tess. You're trusting me the most. You're risking it all. You're betting on the underdog."

"And she's about to win big!" Marvin announced. His deep voice and cool tone cut dramatically into Billy's statement and caused everyone to laugh or cheer in agreement.

Billy and I smiled and kissed each other.

"Listen, thank you all for being here. I love you all, even the ones I just met today."

Everyone laughed again, and my dad used the opportunity to step in and say a few things.

He told the whole story about how he tried to send me to Galveston for the summer so that I would stop making these big plans to move somewhere crazy, like out to California. He told them about moving me down to Galveston, and seeing instantly how happy I was. Then he told the part about me calling home and telling them about Billy.

"I knew after that phone call they'd be getting married. I told her mom that would be the next call we were getting, and it was. And I look at these paintings she comes up with. I see through them that she's happy. I see that she finds beauty, and life, and love in her surroundings down there. And as hard as it is for me to just let her go start a life in an entirely different state, I just know everything's going to be okay. I know she's in the right place." Dad paused and looked at me. "I believe two or three of these paintings are already accounted for, is that right?"

I nodded since Matty had bought three of them before he left.

"But the others are for sale," my dad added, looking at everyone else. "I'd swipe one of these up if you'd like to get your hands on a piece of Tess's art before she gets too famous and we can't afford it anymore."

Chapter 19

Billy

Five months later

Billy would compete in the National Golden Gloves tournament in Kansas City at the end of March, which was two-months' time.

That would be a milestone for him.

But before then, in just two short days, he would box in his eighth amateur match, and his final sanctioned bout before he concentrated his efforts on training for the Golden Gloves.

Billy had escaped from most of his matches unscathed and was able to get back into the ring quickly. His opponent this weekend would be the toughest guy he had faced yet, but Billy still had every intention of coming out of it with an easy victory.

He wasn't full of himself, but he did feel like he was destined for great things. The difference in these two things was subtle, but it meant everything. Billy was extremely confident in his own abilities, but his heart was humble and thankful, and that sort of confidence was endearing.

So, he was feeling pretty good. He was liking his life—liking his prospects. He was excited about the Golden Gloves in a couple of months, and he thought he had a good chance of being a national champion.

Billy had continued to work construction for Matty until a week or so ago, but he had just quit so that he could focus full-time on his boxing career. He did some work for Marvin at the gym, and he worked a couple of hours a day at the hardware store, but the construction he was doing for Matty was back breaking work, and Billy was putting his body at risk when it wasn't necessary. Between their jobs at the hardware store, and Tess selling a few paintings, they were making enough to pay bills and save a little.

Billy focused all of his mental power on becoming a world champion. He studied fight footage and practiced constantly. Even when he wasn't at the gym, he was practicing footwork, shadowboxing, or randomly doing push-ups or sit-ups in their apartment. Tess had thought she married a champion, and Billy would stop at nothing to become one for her.

At this very moment, Billy was going to his old neighborhood for a meeting with Matty. Matty had come to the hardware store and asked Billy to come see him at his house that evening. Billy agreed and said he'd go by there before he headed to the gym.

"There's the man," Matty said as Billy walked toward his front porch.

Matty stood up and shook Billy's hand. The two men had known each other for years. Their familiarity went way back.

It was a beautiful afternoon, warm for the time of year, but Matty led Billy inside, which meant he had something private he wanted to discuss.

They went into Matty's kitchen, toward the barstools, like they so often had in the past.

"What can I get you to drink?" Matty asked.

"It's okay, I have a big jug of water in my car," Billy said. "Thank you, though."

"You've been on a tear," Matty said, walking around Billy and sitting on a stool next to him.

"It feels good," Billy agreed as they got settled.

"I think everybody assumes you'll win this next one up in Houston."

"I think I will," Billy said. "I don't know about everybody else."

"Well, everybody thinks you will. That's why our odds are so good right now."

"Oh, well, that's good news, I guess."

"Very good news," Matty said.

Billy could tell by Matty's tone and his mischievous smile that something was going on— that he was scheming.

"I'm not throwing a fight, if that's what you're getting at, Matty."

Matty flinched at Billy's candid statement. "You say it like I'm asking you to throw a world championship," Matty said lightheartedly. "I wouldn't ask you to do anything big like that. But this is… this is just a little amateur bout, Billy. And it's one that everybody assumes you'll win. I'm telling you, this could be a goldmine if we do it right. If we plan and execute it just right, we stand to make a lot of money here. Enough to get you out of that little apartment. I think it's a no-brainer, pad-na. Think about it. There's no reason you can't have a great career and also plan a few financial windfalls. You're good enough, Billy that you can afford to have a few planned losses. Every fighter has a few losses on their record. Yours could just be a little more thought-out."

Matty smiled and winked at Billy.

The whole thing felt like Matty thought he was doing Billy some big favor. Billy felt like blowing his top. He felt betrayed and let down by Matty, but obviously Matty had no idea. He was smiling and looking at Billy like this was the best idea he had ever come up with—like he assumed Billy would be thankful for the opportunity.

Billy told Matty he didn't want to do it, and Matty laughed and went on to say that he had to get over his pride and see the bigger picture.

Billy, again, said he would have to respectfully decline. Matty, again, tried to reason with him from a business standpoint. He talked about the practical aspects of throwing strategic matches over a long, otherwise successful career.

But Billy wouldn't budge about it.

Matty tried for about an hour, working different angles. He was so convinced and adamant that Billy left his house saying that he would think about it. But the truth was, there was no way Billy was throwing a fight. He didn't feel right about it, and he didn't mind being honest with Matty about that.

In fact, now that he thought about it, he should have gotten upset with Matty for asking him to do such a thing. *How could he ask such a thing?*

Billy headed straight for the gym when he left Matty's. He probably should have gone for a walk on the beach to clear his head first, but he drove straight to Bank Street and parked in front of Marvin's gym.

"It's not that he asked me," Billy said, less than a minute later in Marvin's office. "I expect that from him. It's a reasonable plan, business-wise, given my record and everything. It didn't surprise me that Matty wanted to me do it." Billy blinked at Marvin who just sat there listening. "The worst part is that he was fully convinced that I would be onboard." Billy put his hand to his chest. "I wondered what kind of person I used to be that he was actually *shocked* when I told him I didn't want to throw a match. He laughed at first, thinking I was joking. He said the old Billy would have never turned down an opportunity like this." Billy tilted his head at

Marvin. "Is throwing matches just a part of boxing?" he asked. "That's what Matty told me. Is that true?"

Marvin regarded Billy with a serious expression. "I have never thrown a fight a day in my life, boy. Did Matty tell you to come up here and spill your guts to me like you're doing right now? Did he tell you to ask *me* about it?"

Billy opened his mouth, but hesitated. "W-well, no."

"Then it's not part of boxing," Marvin said. "If you gotta go in some shady corner to talk about something, then that tells you there's a problem."

"I knew that. I wasn't going to do it. I told him that right away when he brought it up. He just kept acting like I was being silly—like it was just part of being a boxer. I knew it wasn't right, but I just can't believe Matty would try to manipulate me like that."

"It's not personal," Marvin said. "Some people, when they're obsessed with something, they lock onto that thing, and they can end up unintentionally hurting people they love because they're so focused on getting it. Matty's locked onto money. He's thinking about nothing but that payday, and he can't appreciate that you might get caught in the crosshairs—that your feelings might be involved. He probably thinks you'd jump at the chance to get paid."

"He *did* think that. He was shocked when I refused."

"I'm sorry, Billy," Marvin said.

Billy thought he would say more, but he just stopped after that and stared at Billy with empathetic eyes.

"Sorry for what?" Billy asked.

"That he's gonna go and let you down like that."

"It's okay," Billy said.

"No, it's not. You've got a match this weekend, and you don't need to think about anything but winning it. You'll win this weekend, and then you're going to nationals in March, and guess what? You'll win there, too."

"That's what I thought," Billy said, standing up with a sigh. "I just wanted to make sure with you in case you were like, *oh, yeah, fighters throw matches all the time*."

"That is one thing you will never, ever hear me say. Now, go get changed, and grab your gloves and jump rope."

Billy smiled. "Yes, sir," he said as he turned to head for the door.

***

It was three hours later when Billy opened the door to his apartment.

It smelled like Tess was making dinner, and he smiled because he was starving. He had gone hard just now. Coach Marvin was good at wearing fighters out when they had something on their mind. When someone wasn't feeling right, he'd say all they needed was to 'sweat it out'. That was a phrase Marvin used quite a bit when he was putting an athlete through a difficult workout, and he said it more than once to Billy today.

Billy was spent. He had broken about four sweats, and it was amazing to walk into his apartment and find that it smelled like delicious food.

He set down his bag and slipped off his shoes by the door. He went to the kitchen, fully prepared to see his wife standing there since it smelled so good. She wasn't in the kitchen, though. It was empty.

Billy went to the fridge to get a drink. He normally drank water, but they kept juice in there because it tasted so amazing after a hard workout. He poured a half glass of apple juice and drank it down in one gulp before rinsing his glass and setting it on the counter for later.

"Hey," Tess said, coming in behind him.

"Hey," he said, turning, taking her in.

Her hair was pulled into a ponytail with her long bangs clipped to the side. She had a painter's apron on and she was barefoot. She smiled as she stepped forward and leaned in to kiss him.

"I don't want to get too close. I might have some wet paint on my apron."

He leaned down to kiss her, lips only. "I stink, anyway."

"I like it when you smell sweaty," she said, leaning up, kissing him again. She licked her lips. "You taste like juice and salt from sweat."

"I'm about to taste better after I take a shower."

"Speaking of taste..." Tess turned and stepped in front of the stove. She opened the pot and began to stir, taking a whiff. "It's my best one yet."

"It smells amazing. What is it?"

"Steak and gravy. There's rice, too. And peas. But they came out a little mushy."

"Peas are mushy," he said. "I didn't think they could come out any other way."

Tess laughed, and Billy touched his stomach. "I'm starving."

"You want some mushy peas?"

"No, I want some steak. How about you give me a bite real quick before I go take a shower?"

Tess smiled and turned to the pot to look for a reasonable bite size piece steak. She had already cut the meat before she let it simmer in the gravy. She balanced a piece on the spoon let it cool for a few seconds before she held it out for him.

Billy ate the bite, feeling so grateful that he got to come home to a beautiful, paint-smeared wife who fed him steak on a spoon and told him his sweat smelled good.

"Thank you," he said. "I love you all the way around the whole world."

"Ahh, so steak makes you sweet," she said, nodding wryly as if she was going to log that one away. She grinned leaned up and kissed him on the cheek. "I love you too," she added, covering the pot again.

"Matty asked me to fix a fight," Billy said.

193

He told Tess everything, so he knew it was just a matter of time before he mentioned it. He figured why not now since it was on his mind.

"You're kidding," she said, turning to stare at Billy.

He shook his head. "I wish I was."

"You didn't beat him up, did you?" she asked, looking concerned.

"No," Billy said chuckling a little. "But I'm glad to hear you assume I might want to. Matty thought I'd be happy to do it with all the money that stands to be made."

"It's not a professional fight," Tess said, wearing a look of confusion. "You're not even getting paid."

"Yeah, but there's still money to be made," he said. "People still bet on amateur fights, and I'm the favorite to win."

"So, if you lost on purpose, Matty would make money?"

"And me, potentially," Billy said.

"What did you say?" she asked.

"I said 'no'. But he's stuck on the idea. He wasn't really hearing me. He's going to bug me about it again."

"Well, lots of people bug us for lots of things in life. There's a customer at the hardware store, Mrs. Olsen, who bugs me to give her half off her order every time she comes in." Tess shrugged. "Sometimes, you just have to disappoint people."

194

Chapter 20

Tess

Two months later
Late March

Golden Gloves National Championships
Kansas City, Kansas

I took a camera with me on our trip to Kansas. I never knew what memories I'd want to paint in the future, so I always took pictures when I didn't have time to sketch my favorite scenes.

Billy had been boxing for less than a year, so some people didn't expect him to fare well at the national tournament, but I knew he would be fine. Golden Gloves was an amateur tournament, and Billy planned on going pro before the next year's contest rolled around. It would be his only year to compete.

So far, he had competed in eight amateur fights and a regional tournament. He did well in all of them, and Marvin didn't hesitate to put him in the open division at Nationals.

Billy was one of four fighters from Bank Street Boxing that made the trip from the coast of Texas to

Kansas City for the tournament. He was the only one who competed in the middleweight division. He was also the only one who made it to the finals.

It was undoubtedly the largest crowd Billy had ever fought in front of. There were thousands of people in attendance for the finals.

The tournament had taken place over the last few days. It was hard to believe we were at the end and it would be over after one last match.

I was more nervous than ever and I prepared myself for Billy to come out. There was one more match to go before his, and I was already shaking with nerves and adrenaline. I took a picture of the ring and the crowd from my seat. My mom and dad were there with me, but Abigail had finals, so she stayed back in Lake Charles.

"Here we are," my dad said, coming back to sit with us after a restroom and refreshment break. He bought popcorn, and my mom reached out for the bag so that Dad could get settled in his seat. Billy was in the back. There was another match before his, but it was getting close to time, and I was so anxious that it was laughable to me that my dad could do something casual like purchase and eat popcorn.

I reached over and took a few pieces from the top of the bag, putting them in my mouth and chewing, just to make sure my basic body functions were even still working.

Billy had come so far. He had fought several times this weekend to get to this match, and I really wanted to see him win.

My dad leaned over my mother so that he could speak to me. He reached out and took the popcorn bag from her in the process.

"I heard a guy behind me in line talking all about Billy," Dad said.

"What'd he say?" I asked, leaning toward him.

"All kinds of stuff. He was talking about how good he was—talking about his speed." He took a handful of popcorn, tossing some of it into his mouth before chewing.

"What about it?" I asked, feeling nervous and desperate for more of the story. "What about Billy's speed? What'd he say?" I ate another bite of popcorn to make myself shut-up.

"He was talking good about Billy," Dad said. "Saying he's really fast for being a bigger fighter. He said people think it's all about strength, but it's not." Dad ate casually as he recited the story, chomping bites between sentences. "He said these guys are all strong, you know. They're all fighters. They all train and lift weights, and let's face it, you have to be born with a certain amount of physical strength to be doing this in the first place. So, it's their speed that sets them apart. That's what he was saying, at least. He said when you think about greats like Ali, it's that they have speed *in addition* to strength." My dad said it dramatically like he really knew what he was talking about.

"So, he was comparing Billy to Ali?" I asked, feeling excited.

Dad nodded and popped a few more kernels excitedly. "He'd been following Billy. He's the one who brought him up."

"Well, did you tell him he was your son-in-law?" Mom asked with wide eyes directed to Dad.

"Of course I did, honey," Dad said. "He stood there and talked about Billy, not even a foot behind me, so of course I turned and introduced myself. I was glad he was being nice, otherwise I might've had cross words."

"What'd he say after you told him who you were?" I asked.

"He complimented Billy again—said he'd probably have a long career."

"I told him he just started boxing a year ago, and he couldn't believe it. He said some really nice things. He's impressed with Billy, and like I said, I wasn't even the one who brought it up."

***

I sat there on pins and needles while we watched the next match. I talked to my parents and even said a few things to Dizzy's wife who was sitting in the chair next to me, but I was out-of-it with nerves and excitement.

I kept thinking about Billy—how much his life had changed in a year. He went from making threats in alleys to competing in one of the most prestigious boxing championships in the world.

Minutes seemed like hours as I waited for Billy's match.

And then it was time.

His name was announced and he walked up the path that led to the ring. I kept praying for him—that he would be strong and fast, like that man said. I just kept thinking to myself that he was the fastest, strongest, best boxer in the whole world.

He walked out with Marvin and Dizzy behind him. I did not take my eyes off of Billy the whole time. I smiled and looked confident so that I would provide a source of encouragement if he happened to glance at me.

He usually did look for me. He usually tried to find me in the crowd. He knew where I had been sitting during the tournament, so I waited for him to glance my way. Finally, his eyes met mine. He didn't smile, but his head moved upward just enough that I knew he had seen me.

I smiled and blew him a kiss.

I hoped he saw me do it. I thought he had, but he was in the process of getting into the ring, and he and Marvin were doing all the things boxers and trainers did before a match.

I had seen them go through this process more than a few times. They had certain things they did ritualistically. Marvin did a lot of talking to Billy, and Billy listened and occasionally nodded. He was wearing white shorts with a black stripe. His shoes and socks were a combination of white and black. He looked understated, not flashy like the colors some of the other guys chose. Billy was a classic. He looked calm and loose and, well… easy.

I did not take my eyes off him. I couldn't. He turned as the announcer was introducing his opponent. His opponent was in black shorts with red trim, but that was all I knew. I didn't pay attention to his name or the announcement at all.

Dizzy was standing behind Billy. He was on the edge of the ring, on the other side of the ropes, and he sprayed a sip of water into Billy's mouth from a plastic water bottle. Billy drank it down, and watching him do it made me remember to breathe. I took a breath in, but then I held it again when Billy looked my way. He scanned the audience as he turned. He saw me, I knew he did. His eyes only stayed on mine for a second, but he saw me.

I didn't even hear his name. The announcer must've said it because everyone around me cheered. Obviously, so did I. I cupped my hands to my mouth, yelling Billy's name in my best cheerleader voice. I yelled for him at every fight. I was not a quiet spectator. I had been around some obnoxious supporters, and I wasn't one of those, but I was a yeller, make no mistake of it.

And just like that, the bell rang and the athletes went to work.

They circled for a few steps, but there was an exchange right off the bat.

Billy's opponent advanced, and Billy got hit on the side of the face. He answered back with a straight jab that made the other guy's head snap back. That one drew gasps from the crowd.

I put my closed fists in front of my face, hiding behind them, waiting to see what would happen next. They had come out, guns blazing. It was fast paced and they were both hitting hard. It was their last match of the tournament, and probably their last amateur match at all.

I flinched at another exchange, and then another.

They barely had time to reset before someone would attack again. They were big boys, and they hit hard. I had seen Billy against a couple of other good guys, but nothing like this.

I was incapable of complex thought.

I thought in small, reactive words.

My internal dialogue sounded like,

go, go, go, go,

yes, yes,

do it,

hit, yes,

block, punch,

oh, block, Billy, block,

yes, go.

There were also little moans and groans that came out of my mouth every now and then when

Billy would get hit or come out on the losing end of an exchange.

I had already learned the following fact about myself:

In fights, I tended to assume Billy was doing worse than he was. I always overemphasized the times he would get hit and underestimated the times he would hit his opponent. It was just the way my brain worked. Seeing Billy get hit made a larger impact on me.

By that reasoning, it seemed to me that Billy was winning this match.

Three minutes passed, the first round ended, and to me, it felt pretty even. But I told myself that if it felt even, it meant that Billy was winning.

"He won that round," Dad said, leaning over Mom.

I glanced at him. "Do you think so? I was thinking that, too."

"Oh, he did," Mom said, nodding.

"That other guy's already getting tired, you can tell," Dad added. "If he keeps it up at this pace, he'll win for sure."

I barely had time to take a deep breath before Billy was standing up again. Marvin spoke to him, getting right in his face. Billy nodded. His eyebrow was cut. There had been blood on his face before Dizzy wiped it off. The other guy looked worse though. *Didn't he?* I glanced toward the other corner, but the other guy's coach was standing in the way and I couldn't see him. I said a prayer for my husband.

And, just like that, the bell rang again.

Second by second, blow by blow, I sat there and watched.

Round two went much like round one.

There was one exciting exchange after another.

I vaguely heard the crowd reacting. I mostly just heard white noise in my own ears. It was too close. It was closer than any fight he had so far.

That other guy was swinging for the fences, just letting hammers fly, and one time, Billy got clipped with one of them, and it caused him to stumble. That happened in the last minute of the second round, and I wasn't sure he had fully recovered by the time the bell rang.

I was praying harder than ever when he went back to his corner.

"He won that, too," Dad said, leaning over Mom again.

He was smiling. *How could he be smiling?*

"Didn't you see him get hit? Didn't you see him start stumbling?"

"Yeah but the other guy got hit a lot more," Dad said. "They go on points. It doesn't matter if Billy got hurt. All that matters is that he scored a lot more points than the other guy that round."

I didn't see how it was possible that Billy scored more points. To me, it seemed like he was getting hit a lot. I told myself I had to trust my dad—that my version of the fight was skewed.

I hated that he had gotten hurt. He was such a good fighter that I had rarely seen him up against someone who was capable of doing that to him.

I barely breathed for the rest of the match.

I stared at Billy, watching his every move.

To me, it seemed that he was the toughest person in the entire world. He took some hits during this match, though. This guy was the best he had ever faced.

But Billy never slowed.

He kept on pushing, answering every blow with two or three of his own. One time, the referee stopped the action so that he could check on Billy's opponent and make sure he could continue.

By the final minutes, I knew that Billy had come out on top. I hadn't counted points like my father and the judges were doing, but I knew that unless something crazy happened, Billy had the match won.

There were only twenty seconds left when Billy landed an overhand right that made the referee call it the match.

He stepped between Billy and the other guy, and Billy easily relented, turning and heading back to his corner, knowing he won. He did the thing he always did. He didn't raise his arms all the way like a lot of boxers did. Billy did a half raise where he lifted his arms from the elbows up and flexed with contained excitement.

Marvin went into the ring and so did Dizzy. They met Billy in the corner and instantly began celebrating by patting him, rubbing his shoulders, and saying things to him.

Billy wore a half-smile and nodded, still looking loose and in the zone. He took a second to go check on his opponent and shake hands with the opposing coaches.

The crowd cheered when Billy came back to our side of the ring, and I raised up my camera and took a picture since the whole scene was almost too overwhelming to look at with my own eyes.

Billy looked at me right when I snapped the photo. I wasn't sure if it would come across on the film or not, but I definitely took the picture when he was looking my way. I was looking through the little viewfinder, taking in the whole composition while zeroing in on his face. I snapped the photo and then I lowered the camera so that I could smile at him with my own eyes.

I blew him a huge kiss with my free hand, and he smiled and lifted his glove at me. There was a celebration in the stands as we waited for them to announce Billy as the champ and gave him his belt.

Billy got my attention and gestured for me to come to him, so I walked toward the ringside area to be there when he finished. It was like I was in a dream. He was at the very beginning of his career and he was already a national champion. The finals match and the moments surrounding his victory were a surreal experience.

Billy caught sight of me coming his way and locked eyes with me until I made it to the corner of the ring and climbed the steps. He leaned in to put his head close to mine when I got there.

"I love you," I said.

Billy propped himself on the rope as he leaned in to kiss me on the mouth. He tasted like battle.

"I love you too," he said.

Epilogue

Two years later

March, 1971

Billy was unstoppable.

Once he started winning and doing post-match interviews, people fell in love with his quiet, likeable demeanor and his handsome boyish looks. His popularity grew, and so did his earnings. He was able to fully quit the hardware store within the first six months of fighting professionally, and his earnings seemed to grow exponentially from there.

We had no bills besides rent and utilities, which were affordable. I was still working at the hardware store, but I had gone down to part-time, and I really only worked there because I liked the job and I liked the Kings. They also ordered canvas for me whenever I needed it and sold it to me at cost. It was convenient, I didn't mind the work, and I had met several art customers through the store.

In fact, that was exactly what I was doing at the moment. I was currently delivering one of my paintings to its new home, and it was going to a friend of Mr. King.

It was a colorful painting of the boardwalk at night. The man commissioned it, size and subject matter. I had painted a daytime boardwalk scene, so I knew I would enjoy it, but the difference in this commission and others I had done was that he wanted it so large. It was on a canvas that was three feet tall and six feet wide.

Billy had to help me build the canvas. I had been working on this one painting for two whole weeks straight. That might not seem like a long time in the grand scheme of things, but I was accustomed to having several works in progress and working quickly and efficiently, so this was an intense project for me.

The buyers had a gorgeous, ornate frame custom built and I had already installed it on the painting. I was absolutely in love with the finished product. It was grand.

I painted it in our bedroom (which was also my studio, although I didn't go around announcing that to my customers). It seemed to take up the whole room, especially once we installed it into the frame.

It was gorgeous. I was thankful someone had commissioned such a piece, but at the same time I was sad to see it go. It reminded me of that first dance with Billy where I told Jacob Collier to go kick a tin can.

Billy had told me nothing was stopping me from painting another one just like it. He was right, and I knew it, but I still complained about parting ways with this one—especially once I saw it in the frame.

I'd be sad to see it go, and that would happen within moments.

I was currently at the location.

I borrowed Mr. King's delivery van to transport the painting to its new home. Randall and Kenny had helped me load it up. I knew I would have help unloading it once I got onsite, so I made the delivery alone.

The address took me to a large, two-story, aqua-blue Victorian house on the corner of Bank Street and 17th. It was only about six blocks from the hardware store.

The Connors were parked in the driveway. I knew that because they had gotten out of their car and were waiting for me. The Connors owned the frame shop. They were the ones who had designed and built the frame. I pulled into the driveway and parked behind them.

"Are you guys the ones here to help me unload and hang this?" I asked, "Or..." I hesitated. "This isn't your house... is it?"

I suddenly felt a little confused, and the feeling only grew when I saw Mrs. Connor's confused face.

"We don't really even know what we were doing here," she said. "We had a guy call the store, asking if we could help hang a painting at this address. We didn't even know what painting we were hanging."

"I guess it's mine," I said.

"That big one?" Mr. Connor asked, his eyebrows raised.

I nodded, and he whistled like we were in for a job.

"Is there hardware on it yet?" he asked.

"Yes, sir. I put a wire on it."

"Is it secure?" he asked. "Because that frame alone is fifty pounds."

"It's secure," I said, nodding. "Billy and Mr. King helped me with it."

I glanced at the house. "Are the people here?"

"No. We knocked. There's an envelope taped on the door, but nobody answered."

I walked to the door, looking around, noticing the envelope, which was blank. I knocked, cautiously at first and then a little louder. I turned and made a face at the Connors who had come up to stand behind me.

"I'm just going to try the envelope," I said.

I opened it, and there was a handwritten note with two words.

Come inside.

There was also a key.

I unlocked the door and opened it.

"It's empty," I said, looking around and noticing that the house was completely vacant. My words echoed.

"Look," Mrs. Connor said. She pointed, and I followed her gesture to the far wall in the entryway. There was a piece of paper hanging on the wall, and we all made our way over to it.

Please hang the painting on this wall.
Let the artist choose the positioning.
We trust her.

I looked at Mrs. Connor with a shrug. "I guess they trust me," I said. I pointed at the wall where it was to be hung. It was painted a soft blue-grey color that would go perfectly with the painting. I knew it would look amazing there.

"It's going to be easy to center on that wall," I said. "It's just a matter of how high or low."

I didn't second guess myself. I worked quickly with the Connors to haul in the painting and hang it. It took us the better part of an hour, but it was worth it.

I stood back, shaking my head at myself for wanting to keep this thing in my bedroom when it so obviously belonged in a house like this. I didn't always get to see my paintings after they were hung, and I was thankful I got to see this one in its new home.

Mr. and Mrs. Connor loved how the whole thing came out. Mrs. Connor asked me about five times for the name of the guy who had bought it so she could call his wife and come by and take a photograph once furniture was in the home. She said she wanted to use it for advertising for their shop. I told her I had set everything up through Nathaniel King since the family was a friend of his.

I promised her I would get the person's name, and they took off. They left so quickly that it took me a second to realize I was stuck with a decision to make about the key. I didn't know whether I should lock the house and tape the key back onto the door, or leave the house open and leave the key inside.

My first thought was to call Nathaniel and ask him what to do.

I glanced around in the next room, looking for a telephone, but there was nothing. I decided I would leave the key inside, near the painting, and leave the door unlocked. I was on my way back to the hardware store, anyway. I could have Nathaniel call the guy and tell him the painting was in place and the key was inside the house.

I placed the key neatly in the envelope on the floor underneath the painting.

I was on my way out when I opened the door and ran into Billy. My face instantly changed to one of confusion. I glanced behind Billy to see the Connor's car driving away.

"Hey," I said, feeling a little confused. "I thought you were working out. Are you okay?"

"Yeah, yeah, I'm fine," he said. "I was just coming to check on you... to see how the painting looked once you got it up."

"Oh, gosh, Billy, perfect timing," I said. I took a step back, smiling and letting him in. "You need to come in here and see this!"

He followed me inside.

"I didn't expect it to be empty," I said. "But that made it easy to hang. Mr. Connor had a ladder, thank goodness. There wasn't one in the van, and I didn't even think about that. Mrs. Connor's going to contact these people to see if she can get a photograph of it once they have their furniture in here. I'll probably get a copy. Isn't it amazing on this wall?"

We had come to stand in front of the painting as I was talking, and we both looked up at it.

"Are you sad to see it go?" Billy asked.

"I thought I'd be sadder than I am, honestly," I said. "Seeing it here on this wall makes me happy." I looked all around. "It looks so good in this house."

"It's yours, Tess."

Billy spoke slowly and seriously enough that I glanced at him with a look of disbelief and confusion. My heart pounded.

"I bought the painting," Billy said with a little smile and nod.

"Are you serious?" I asked with wide eyes.

He nodded again. I could tell by the way he stared at me that he was serious.

My eyes began to sting. I was trying to see the positive by admiring the painting in its new home, but the truth was, I'd rather own it for myself than sell it to someone else.

"You bought it back from this guy?" I asked excitedly. "What do we do now? Just take it down and put it in the van again? I wish I would have known. We put nails in their wall already, but I guess maybe he'll hang something else there."

Billy smiled and put his hand around my waist, pulling me in. "Your wall."

"What?"

"You really don't get it yet?" he said.

"Get what?"

"We don't have to move the painting, Tess."

"I thought you said you bought it back."

"I didn't buy it back. I bought it the first time. I also bought the house." He grinned. "Welcome home."

He was speaking so quietly and calmly, that my brain didn't quite understand. My eyes really started stinging, and I blinked. Billy said he bought the house. *Could he mean this house? He said he bought the painting, and then he said he also bought the house.*

It was too hard to believe.

We had been living in that apartment on Bank Street for three years, and I had never thought of moving. I had never even mentioned it.

My heart began pounding as Billy's words sank in. I went limp. I was only pretending to faint, but

Billy caught me in his arms, laughing, knowing I was joking.

"Are you serious?" I asked slowly.

"Yes."

"Is this whole entire house *ours*?"

"Yes."

"You bought it?"

"Yes."

"And the painting, too?"

"Well, y-yes," Billy said, laughing a little like that was an afterthought.

We were standing in the entryway of the most beautiful home I had ever seen, and it was mine. It was perfect. It was unexpected. I was speechless. I was so full of shock and emotion that I didn't know what to say or even feel first.

"Thank you," I said, figuring that was a good place to start.

Billy pulled me closer. "You're welcome," he returned. He rested his hand on my back. His arms were around me, holding me. He was solid and strong. He was in peak physical condition, and I always loved to gently touch his muscles and trace the shapes of them. Billy loved it when I did that. I let my fingertips move over his shirt, tracing the hard ridges of his wide, muscular back.

Billy stared at me with a mischievous grin. "You wanna go check out the upstairs before I head back to the gym?"

Billy was a bad boy from way back, and I knew what he was asking.

"Of course I do," I said. "Are you sure this is my house, though?"

Billy grinned. "We wouldn't be having this conversation if it wasn't."

"So, it is? It's mine? Ours?"

"Yes. We can move in today if we want."

I glanced around, feeling awestruck, speechless. "I had no idea," I said.

"That's what makes it so fun," Billy said.

And then he kissed me.

Billy's soft mouth touched mine, and all was right with the world. It was flawless. All of it—the whole moment was so very good, the sounds and the smells, the taste of Billy's kiss, the painting, the house. Everything about it was perfect.

The two of us would settle into that house on the corner of Bank Street and 17th and stay there for years to come.

The End
(till book 2)

Thanks for reading Easy Does It. Bank Street Stories is a multi-generational series that will keep up with Tess and Billy and star some of their family and friends. Books 2 through 9 are available now.

God bless and happy reading!

Thanks to my team ~ Chris, Coda, Jan, Glenda and Yvette

Made in the USA
Middletown, DE
31 October 2021